LOPEZ'S LOOT

They were cousins, riding partners: Drifter, a white American, and Lopez — half-Mexican, travelling the southern border trails of the USA. Their money-raising schemes were often shady, sharing the risks and rewards: like the time Drifter turned in his 'wanted' partner, Lopez, and later sprung him. However, things changed when loot, in the form of church treasures, came their way. Clashing with posses and renegades their lives were at risk. Could they ever gain a more settled way of life?

DAVID BINGLEY

◆

LOPEZ'S LOOT

Complete and Unabridged

LINFORD
Leicester

First published in Great Britain in 1975

First Linford Edition
published 2010

The moral right of the author has been asserted

British Library CIP Data

Bingley, David, *1920* –
    Lopez's loot.- -(Linford western library)
    1. Western stories.
    2. Large type books.
    I. Title II. Series
    823.9'14–dc22

ISBN 978–1–44480–202–3

Published by
F. A. Thorpe (Publishing)
Anstey, Leicestershire

Set by Words & Graphics Ltd.
Anstey, Leicestershire
Printed and bound in Great Britain by
T. J. International Ltd., Padstow, Cornwall

This book is printed on acid-free paper

1 ✳

At five o'clock in the afternoon, the air was still and heavy in a bright blue sky to the south of Pecos County, Texas. Here and there, in the widespread meadows of sparse yellowing grass, lean beeves belonging to the Hacienda Abello bawled briefly, expressing bovine disapproval of the fodder under their feet and the myriad flies which seemed to thrive about them under the sultry border country sun.

In the shade of the peeling buildings, bulky men of mixed Mexican and Texan blood availed themselves of every patch of shade and snoozed, even though the time allowed for *siesta* by Señora Abello who ran the *rancho*, was long since past.

In a stable, a young man who should have been helping to shoe horses was playing a guitar. Other hands, and some riders who were resting before drifting through to other parts, were engaged in games of chance in the bunkhouse.

Some two hundred yards to the north-west of the buildings was a roughly ploughed kitchen garden spanned by uneven furrows of brown soil. During most of that morning and part of the afternoon, a tall lean young man, stripped to the waist apart from a broad-brimmed flat-crowned dun stetson, had been lifting potatoes and putting them in sacks to a weight around one hundred and thirty pounds.

He had eaten and slept through the most oppressive heat of the day, and now, late in the afternoon he was bent upon a bit of target practice. Across one end of the garden, between seventy and eighty yards away, he had sus-pended the sacks by ropes tightly tied around the necks. The suspending ropes were looped over a substantial horizon-tal rope stretched taut between two wooden posts some fifty feet apart and eight feet above the ground.

2

The young man, a white American in his middle twenties, squinted at the slowly turning sacks from the scant shade of a couple of dwarf oak trees at the other end of the furrows. He had thrust muscular arms through the rolled-up sleeves of his red shirt and knotted a blue bandanna about his neck before taking up his stance facing the sacks.

He toyed with a nicely-balanced Winchester repeating rifle as though savouring the action to come. A faint smile played about the corners of his wide mouth and the premature crows-feet wrinkles at the outer ends of his green eyes.

The butt of a home-rolled cigarette was removed from his mouth and rubbed out on his boot sole. He tilted his hat forward to shade his eyes still more and gently stroked the close-cropped auburn beard which linked his sideburns along the lines of his jaw and chin.

He advanced his left shoulder and

carefully set his feet, moving as if he was long accustomed to firearms discharged from the shoulder. His left eye closed as he peered along the barrel and sighted the weapon on one of the ropes suspending a sack. He licked his lips as though reluctant to press the trigger.

Almost as an afterthought, he shifted to another target and casually shot a large splinter out of the supporting posts. His breathing became more regular, as if one casual inconsequential bullet had purged him of an attack of nerves.

Muscles worked on the sides of his jaw as he lined up again on the first of the suspended six sacks. His index finger tightened slowly on the trigger. The Winchester kicked and a sack slumped to the earth in an eddying cloud of dust. He levered, shifted his aim and banged off again, with the same result.

The echoes of his third success were still dinning in his ears when he was distracted. Someone was anxiously calling his name. He frowned, flaring his nostrils and with some apparent effort took his attention off the sacks. Hurrying alongside of the dry-stone boundary wall was the bulky rolling figure of Carmelita Abello, the Mexican rancher's wife, and she looked troubled.

Like many men who lived near the border with Mexico, Esteban Abello was often away from home on 'business.' So it was that Carmelita virtually ran the *rancho* at all times. At forty years of age, she had more energy than both her teenage sons put together. She had run to fat in the previous ten years, and still she always walked as though about to break into a run.

She was dressed as always in a soiled grey work frock topped by a black apron. Her round, seamed troubled face was framed by long black greying hair parted in the middle. Her eyes were as black as jet.

'Ah, there you are, Señor Drifter! I should have known when I heard the bang of your gun! Come with me, I beg you. We have trouble. Your cousin, Lopez, is making it. In the bunkhouse with my boys, Felipe and Velasco and some of the wandering riders who are visiting with us.'

The man who answered to Drifter nodded. 'Lopez is fightin' again, I guess. And too full of liquor for his own good. Land's sakes, some guys jest don't know how to conduct themselves when they're visiting with a respectable Mexican family who treat them like blood relations. Lopez sure is darned embarrassin' at times. I'll come along right away.'

Drifter tucked in his shirt, cradled his rifle and fell into step beside the Mexican woman whose anger was already fading due to the Texan's flattery.

'Lopez is jest no good in drink, Carmelita, an' that's a fact!'

'I know, I know, Señor Drifter, but perhaps it is partly my fault. As you know it was my Felipe's birthday yesterday an' I left a lot of liquor in the ranch house. When they drink too much they don't know what they do. But if you will stop them, Señor Drifter an' send my hands about their business. It is time we forget the birthday now an' get down to some serious work.'

As the two of them drew steadily nearer to the bunk-house, two voices in particular, arguing loudly in Spanish, stood out above the general clamour. One was that of Lopez, Drifter's cousin, and the other belonged to a tall lean long-necked Mexican with smouldering eyes who was one of the men just passing through.

Drifter shifted the grip on his weapon and edged ahead of the woman. He knew just how far Lopez was likely to go, primed by liquor. The Abello woman had treated them well, and he was anxious that no serious incident should mar the rest of their stay.

The two angry voices were cut short as one man answered the challenge of the other. The silence grew ominous.

Drifter lengthened his stride, so that he was breathless when he kicked open the door and stood a yard inside the building, surveying the tight ring of observers and the fighters in their midst.

Felipe and Velasco, one thin and one fat, had already passed out and were sleeping off their intake of liquor on a pair of bunks against the far wall. On some of the supporting posts, greasy playing cards had been pinned to the woodwork by slim-bladed throwing knives. Other cards were scattered about the floor and benches. But the time of gaming was over.

Scarcely a yard apart, the two contestants in the central area were circling one another, each armed with a knife and each with one end of a red scarf gripped between his teeth.

Drifter's heart thumped as he recovered his breath. He was used to violence and to action of most sorts, but he had never become used to men who threatened each other with knives.

Lopez had discarded his battered steeple hat. His short, black curly hair was flattened across his forehead with perspiration. He weighed a good thirteen stones which was well distributed over his five-feet nine-inch frame. The whites of his brown eyes were an alcoholic pink. His lips were parted in a wolfish grin, baring his gapped teeth as he fought off his drunken haze and endeavoured to outwit his opponent. Patches of perspiration made parts of his grey shirt almost as dark as his swinging leather vest.

Opposite him, the long-necked Hernandez did his circling on slightly bowed legs, his tall hat still in place on his head, his bulbous eyes radiating hatred. The eyes of the observers went from one man to the other, weighing their chances. At thirty-two, Lopez was a few years the older. He was more experienced and looked the craftier of the two, but he had also had more to drink. So, perhaps the contestants were evenly matched.

Señora Abello's heaving bosom against his back prompted Drifter to some sort of action. He had already seen the two knife experts narrowly miss each other a couple of times. Almost at any second blood would flow, and after that the outcome was anyone's guess.

Drifter turned and frowned at her. She was a powerful woman with a lot of influence over men, but their intake of alcohol had ensured that they would be slow to react to her urgent intreaties. There was a sort of pleading in her eyes which a man could not shrug off. Drifter nodded and stepped forward, pushing his tall figure through the throng of men.

Some resented his intrusion, thinking he simply wanted to watch the contest from the front. Others, catching his eye and noticing the rifle which he carried with him, gave way more readily. Even when he had reached the front of the circle, however, there were those who were not even aware of his presence.

Neither of the fighters knew he was

there. He spent a few minutes sizing them up from close quarters, and then he made his move.

'The Señora Abello says this fight has to stop!'

The fighters both managed some sort of hostile noise in their throats. Neither of them could speak for fear of losing his grip on the cloth between them. While Drifter worked his way around the inner edge of the crowd, the knifers glanced out of their eye corners towards the door, where the owner's wife was expected to be.

Behind the watchers, she babbled something almost like an oath in fast elided Spanish. At the same time, Drifter stepped forward. He brought down the barrel of his Winchester with quite a bit of force behind it. It struck the stretched piece of silk about half-way between the two men. As each of them had been trained to withstand pressure on the teeth in this sort of fighting, neither of them lost their grip. In fact, their jaws tightened, with the result that their heads were forcibly drawn together.

Neither expected to be hauled in the direction of his opponent's head quite in that manner: consequently, their skulls cracked together at forehead level, directly above the eyes. While they were still stunned and the watchers were protesting and grumbling in disbelief, Drifter followed up his advantage. With an upward sweep of his rifle, he knocked Hernandez's weapon flying out of his hand. Lopez, recovering quickly in spite of the alcoholic haze, avoided an up-stroke with the barrel, but as he turned his attention to his interfering cousin, he received a kick in the ribs which winded him and made him forget about the knife for the few crucial seconds while his arm was twisted.

Hernandez looked on, angry and weaponless, while Señora Abello elbowed her way forward and took general control. Drifter had to clout his sturdy cousin twice across the jaw before his senses left him. After that, the tension went out of the air. Men who were work-shy shuffled out into the open air and wondered what easy job they could do to pass the hours until sundown.

Five minutes after she arrived, the señora bustled out again, followed by Drifter who had his cousin's limp body slung over his shoulder. The woman called her thanks as the tall Texan stalked off round the back of the building with his human burden. In a dry wooden trough, situated a few feet from a water pump, Drifter dumped the body. The eyes half-opened and then closed even more firmly than before. In a matter of a few seconds, Lopez's plump cheeks were moving in and out as he snored. A slight breeze lifted the hair around the small bald patch on the crown of his head.

Velasco, the slimmer of Señora Abello's two sons, sidled up to the pump where he washed his face and neck and took a drink.

'If you are around in an hour, put the

water on Lopez. Wake him up properly and tell him to come lookin' for me. All right?'

Velasco showed Drifter respect, even though he was only a visitor, and the tall Texan wandered away, thinking seriously about the future.

★ ★ ★

Towards half past six, Lopez revived, made good use of the pump and finally staggered off to seek out his cousin. Drifter was stretched out under an oak in the kitchen garden area with his hands behind his head and his hat pushed forward.

'You wanted to see me cousin.'

No movement from the reclining figure.

'I am sorry about what happened back there in the bunkhouse. It was the liquor. I had a little too much, I guess. You know how it is, Drifter.'

'I know how it is, Lopez, an' I, too, am sorry about your latest incident with

14

the knife. It is time we moved on.'

Lopez puffed his cheeks. He groaned. 'You are very angry with me, amigo, but it will pass. It always has done before. Why don't we think of other matters? After all, we are of the same blood.'

Drifter cleared his throat and pushed back his hat. 'I have been thinkin' of other matters. It's time we moved on. I wasn't jokin'. It is true your father and mine were brothers. Mine married a Texas woman, and yours a Mexican. Sometimes I wonder if there are really any true similarities between us. Other than that we both get restless if we stay in one place too long.'

Lopez spread his hands and bent towards his cousin, his face showing what he thought to be a fetching smile. 'But, amigo, *I* am not restless yet. What is the hurry?'

'It is time,' Drifter returned brusquely. 'The news of that little hold-up job you did in Laredo will have penetrated as far as the nearest town to this spot, Rio

City. We're goin' to Rio, *pronto*!'

Lopez' expression hardened. The poise of his body suggested menace but when Drifter came to his feet with a lithe muscular movement and stared him out he gave ground.

'Go and saddle up our horses, cousin, while I pay the señorita. We shan't be around for the evenin' meal.'

Drifter moved away with a steady even pace. Presently, Lopez headed for the stables.

2

The Hacienda Abello was situated about two to three miles north of the great Rio Grande del Norte river which marked the boundary with Mexico to the south. Rio City, the township which was next on the agenda of Drifter and Lopez, lay in a north-easterly direction from the Mexican border ranch at a distance of between eight and ten miles.

The two riding partners spent nearly three hours after leaving the *rancho* keeping on the move but maintaining a very modest pace. All the time they were moving in the general direction of Rio City; sometimes using old tracks, at other times crossing unbroken ground.

In the first hour, Lopez grumbled a lot as the effects of several days' intake of alcohol began to slowly wear off. For perhaps half an hour after that, he kept asking pointed questions which mostly fell on deaf ears. Finally, for the latter part of the journey he slumped in the saddle of the plodding sweating low-barrelled roan horse which had had the doubtful privilege of carrying him for the past three months.

Neither rider cared very much for the first day of moving on. Both were restless, being creatures of a rather tricky border between two countries which had fought a bitter war not many years before they were born. Their fathers, who were grown men around the time of the Civil War, had been forced to hit the owlhoot trail in the bewildering aftermath of the late 1860s.

Lopez's father, the older of the two brothers, had spent a lot of time in Mexico, where he had married a Mexican woman during a brief period spent in one place. Drifter's father had chosen to face matrimony in Texas with a woman of his own race. So it was that two cousins of the same sex contrived to look so different in spite of a similar outlook in their restless itinerant way of life.

On this occasion, Drifter was heading for a specific place. He did not have the intention of going straight into Rio, the spot where they intended to do business. He was looking for a place to go to earth within comparatively easy riding distance of the settlement and at the same time being isolated.

Only the exact layout of the immediate geography of the spot he sought kept him moving slowly. While Lopez had been spending a lot of his time drinking and gaming at the hacienda, Drifter had taken his chances to question men moving through the county.

Two of them had suggested this secluded valley ahead, with its shack and creek and no obvious track leading into it.

Shortly after nine-thirty that evening, Drifter spotted the line of three leaning pine tree boles on the west side of a ridge and knew he was almost there. He checked his long-legged sorrel, waited for the roan to overtake them and casually kicked his partner's riding boot to prod him into life.

Lopez started visibly, realised in a split second that he was in the saddle, made slight muscular adjustments to keep his balance, went for his twin .44s and then slowed up. They were halfway out of their holsters when his bleary eyes met Drifter's gaze not more than four feet away.

'Shucks, it's you again. It's always you, cousin. I might have known it.' He slid his guns back into leather, blinked and peered around him. 'So where are we?'

Drifter grinned, and rolled a cigarette round to the corner of his mouth with his tongue. 'Have a guess, cousin, why don't you?'

Lopez glowered at him, but he was genuinely curious. He stared forward at the winding path which led through a fault in the ridge, narrowed and almost hidden in parts by bulking rocks and encroaching bushes and plants.

'I don't smell no beer from the saloons, an' my ears don't detect no honkie-tonk piano music for the uplift of ridin' gentry. Tell me, cousin, why in tarnation are we still out in the back of nowhere at this advanced hour of the evening?'

'We're headin' for a hideout, not town. If it's easy to find, it won't serve our purpose. Unless your gamblin' friends have been stringin' me along, it's right on through there, in the valley beyond.'

Lopez grunted, and showed sufficient interest in the immediate future to take the lead for a while. He entered the valley ten minutes later with his back straight, whistling a few bars of a tune which had once been used by the Mexican general Santa Anna, and acting as if all the planning and careful groundwork on this trip had been done exclusively by himself.

They viewed the distant cabin, again almost hidden, this time by trees, from a high point not far beyond the ridge. It was upwards of half a mile away. Showing much more alertness, they cantered down the slope until the distance was halved. After that, they parted company and cautiously went the rest of the way taking advantage of every scrap of cover.

Leaving their mounts some fifty yards away, they completed the distance to the unlighted shack in a style which would not have shamed Indians. They straightened up, one to look through a window, and the other to peer through the half-opened back door, about the same time.

Drifter's were the boots to make the warped floorboards creek. He admitted Lopez at the front a few seconds later. Obviously, no one was using the shack at that time. The smell of dust and old cloying food odours confirmed the evidence in the stove that it had not been inhabited for some weeks, perhaps even months.

For the first time in a couple of weeks

they worked alongside of each other like a smooth, efficient team. The table and the sideboard needed clearing and cleaning. Likewise the loft, where two low bunks were laid out. After that, Lopez tended the stove and the horses while Drifter prepared a frying pan meal from the ample saddle provisions provided by the Abello woman.

Eventually, they stretched out on the twin beds around half past eleven, with a hanging oil lamp swinging through a short arc above their heads. Eddying tobacco smoke made curious patterns as the patch of light came and went.

Lopez said: 'If you're plannin' on goin' into this town on your own tomorrow to ask pointed questions, you could have left me at the Abello ranch for a while longer. I could have made my way here a day or two later.'

'It wouldn't have done, an' you know it. You have to be sober to pull the kind of caper you go in for. Sober before the event, as well as at the time. If you stay here an' rest, an' keep out of mischief till I finish the preliminary work, everything will be all right.'

Drifter's argument had the effect of stirring up some of Lopez's basic bitterness. 'Always you go on about my drunkenness. If I'm such a bad risk, why don't *you* do the robbery part of the act an' get yourself chased, an' let me go along with capturin' you an' winnin' the bounty?'

'You know why we don't do it that way before you ask cousin. *You* do the hold-up because yours is the face on the reward notices. If I did it there'd be no reward money for anyone to collect because I don't have reward dodgers followin' me around. Now, why don't you stop feelin' so bitter about things an' get off to sleep?'

'I haven't let you down this far, an' I reckon you'd have been far worse off if we hadn't teamed up when we did.'

Lopez waved the decreasing butt of a cigar in the air. 'How can you say that? I mean about me bein' worse off if we hadn't teamed up! How can you say that, for goodness' sakes. How can you know?'

Drifter emptied his mouth, throat and lungs of tobacco smoke. He did it with a gentle sigh as if the argument was tiring him unnecessarily.

'I know because in the days before I took to takin' you in for the reward and then settin' you free again, you were a bungler! You often used to go on a job full of beer or whiskey. You used to let yourself be seen an' nearly caught before we decided you should let folks get a glimpse of you as part of our plannin'.

'If you'd gone on alone, you'd have ended up in the penitentiary at Yuma, or some such place, long before this. You'd have big muscles, a poor diet and you'd be wonderin' if you'd be fit enough to want to go on livin' after you had served your time. The prospect would not have been a pleasant one.'

Lopez muttered a few unprintable oaths in Spanish. He tossed about in his bed, hammered his cigar butt into the loft timbers with his fist and gave way to a sudden touch of anger.

'Now look here, cousin, why don't you admit it? Deep down inside you're jest as bitter as I am. My father and your father, they were both no good. They left us without prospects, and here we are. But you have me weighed up as no good, a derelict fit for nothin' an' that's for sure.

'I believe you hate me! If that's true, then how can I be sure you won't leave me in the lurch one of these days? One day soon, you could take me in, draw the reward money an' simply head for the border while I play the main part at a necktie party, or start my long term as a guest in some penitentiary! Will you tell me what I ask? How do I know you won't let me down an' make off with the proceeds for some other state where you ain't known?'

Drifter was so long in answering that Lopez thumped him hard on the bicep with his fist before he replied.

'The short answer is that you don't

know, amigo. In this county, Pecos County, there's only one penalty for robbery with violence. The rope, on account of it being so near the border with Mexico an' tradition dyin' hard.

'You don't know whether I'm likely to leave you in the lurch one day, but what alternative have you? I'm the only kin you know! You don't make friends! But it is true, though, that I'm in some measure the same. I don't have roots. If I left you to pay for your sins in this neck of the woods, I wouldn't know where to go to settle. I have no place an' no people. So try an' gather some comfort from that.

'While you were livin' it up in that bunkhouse back there, I was liftin' potatoes an' other jobs, to help pay for our keep. When I wasn't busy I practised with my Winchester, shootin' through ropes the thickness of those used for hangin' people in this county. And I didn't do that jest because I was gun-happy, either.'

There was a long silence after Drifter

had said his piece. Only Lopez's rather noisy breathing rasped on the silence. The latter's voice sounded very subdued when he started to speak again.

'Drifter, do you think we'll ever strike it big in these small banks an' stores we bust into, or will it all be chicken feed, all along?'

'I guess it'll always be chicken feed with the likes of us, cousin,' Drifter murmured. 'On account of there's safety of sorts in actin' with moderation. If we went for the big stuff, we'd be out of our depth. We'd draw too much attention, attract more law than we could cope with, an' that would put us out of business for good. Both of us.'

Lopez's bed creaked under him as he wriggled to find a more comfortable position. 'Cousin, I know you're the brains behind this twosome, but does it ever occur to you that this is a short term business we're in? That it can't go on forever?'

Lopez stopped talking. Drifter refrained from answering, but he nodded in the gloom, unseen. A few minutes later, Lopez seemed to run a temperature, as if he had a fever or a touch of the border ague. When he started to shiver so uncontrollably that his teeth rattled, Drifter abruptly got up, threw a spare blanket over him, and went down the ladder for a bottle of whiskey which he had intended to keep from his partner indefinitely.

Back in the loft, he pulled the cork and forced the bottle between the stricken man's teeth, About three fingers went down the throat, and a few teaspoonsful more were spilled on the blanket.

Presently, Lopez was restored. Drifter nodded, patted him on the shoulder and put out the light. In the darkness, the tall Texan felt at that moment nothing but sympathy for his unpredictable companion. He knew that the ague was brought on by nothing more than fear. Fear, and uncertainty about the future. It was a deadly sort of fear to have to live with.

3

The following morning was a fine, clear one with the promise of great heat in the offing. Drifter and Lopez rose at an early hour and bathed in the creek before sharing a substantial breakfast. Drifter was calm and thoughtful, while Lopez showed no signs of the malaise of the previous evening. The latter was in a singing mood. He made cheerful jests as his partner swung into the saddle of his sorrel and set off on the journey to Rio City.

Pushed to a useful speed, the reddish-brown horse made short work of the journey to the north. It was a little after ten in the morning when Drifter walked it up the main street of the town, liberally coated in trail dust. The thoughtful green eyes of the new arrival were busy under the broad brim of his dun stetson as he took note of the buildings and the townsfolk ambling about their daily business.

It was a town in two halves. One part of it consisted of adobe dwellings such as were favoured by the Mexican part of the community, and the other of log cabins and board dwellings of the predominantly white Texan element.

Drifter tethered his mount to a hitch outside a big false-fronted saloon named the Border, and strolled through the batwings knocking the dust out of his clothing. His eyes took a little time to accustom themselves to the interior gloom, and he was aware of many curious eyes before a short, stocky barman with a paunch and a bald head confronted him across the long bar and produced beer for him. He drank it down in three long swallows, called for more and took the second offering more leisurely.

He had a cigarette at a jaunty angle in his mouth when he enquired after the whereabouts of the town marshal's office and was directed up the west end of the thoroughfare. A crudely painted wooden shingle on the door announced the name of the peace officer, one Anton O'Halloran.

After knocking on the door, Drifter stepped inside and closed the door behind him. He toyed with his hat while he took stock of the surroundings. There were guns in racks on two walls. The glass in the street window had a long crack in it. The floorboards were pitted with holes as though some earlier official had trailed his feet wearing large Spanish spur wheels.

Marshal O'Halloran had his back to the visitor while another man, very different in appearance, was in the act of tipping a panful of dust out through the grille in the cell wall at the rear.

Smoke from a small cigar eddied round the head and shoulders of the marshal, who was seated at his desk reading a newspaper held open between his arms. The Mexican deputy who had been clearing up sneezed, having tipped away his dust, and was the first to take any notice of Drifter.

'Good day to you both. I'm jest passin' through an' I have a favour to ask.'

Deputy Fuente, a pockmarked, stocky Texican in his middle thirties got rid of the dust pan, blinked, grinned and wiped his hands on the front of his bleached blue shirt. Stubby fingers toyed briefly with his red bandanna and adjusted the fitting of his shapeless undented hat.

'Señor Marshal, we have a visitor.'

The figure sporting a fringed buckskin jacket made the swivel chair creak. Even then, he was slow to turn and look his visitor over. With some show of reluctance, he lowered the newspaper and favoured Drifter with a rather chilly stare.

Drifter was equally observant. He noted that O'Halloran was lean and probably tall, with hollow temples, high cheekbones and a big jaw. The peace officer was clean-shaven. He had a leathery sort of skin. The long hair carefully combed out at the nape of his neck was fair and wavy.

'It's a little early for the type of business this office deals with. What sort of trouble are you in, stranger?'

Drifter grinned. He lowered his hat and shifted his feet on the scarred floor. 'I'm not in any trouble right now. It's information I seek. I think you may be able to help me.'

'What sort of information do you want?' O'Halloran demanded, brusquely.

The deputy scuttled around the room and took up a stance beside the window which looked out onto the street. He was admiring the sorrel, recently hitched outside.

'I'd like to examine your reward notices, if it wouldn't be too much trouble.'

O'Halloran's interest quickened, although his gaze remained bleak.

'You think we have outlaws in this town?'

'I think you might have, marshal. I'm lookin' for the likeness of one man in particular.'

'Describe him,' the peace officer invited.

Drifter put on a gauche expression, and pretended that he did not have the gift of explaining things in words. 'I'd do a whole lot better if I saw a picture of the fellow. Even if it was a poor likeness.'

The marshal opened the drawer where the notices were kept. He then hesitated, forced a grin which emphasised the size of his jaw, and thrust forward a stubby forefinger.

'I wonder what you'd do if you saw your own picture on one of my dodgers!'

Drifter's expression suddenly turned bleak. He drummed across the front of his soiled red shirt with the fingers of his free hand. Abruptly, his interrogator relented, pulled out the documents in question and blew the dust off them. He ordered the deputy to go for a walk, and gestured for Drifter to step closer.

There were about a score of notices all told. As they turned them over, one at a time, the peace officer's hard eyes were never still. Always they travelled between the papers and the face of his visitor. He gave the impression of being a remarkably keen officer who studied his fellow men.

Lopez's likeness, drawn by a moderately good artist to the description given by two or three eye-witnesses, was reasonably good. Drifter's mouth twitched into a hard line. O'Halloran knew at once that this was the special one. He pushed the others aside and squinted at the picture and the words written around it.

Eventually, he turned it over to Drifter, who picked it up and read it very closely.

Lopez, it appeared, was wanted dead or alive, for armed robbery with violence in Pecos County, Texas. Five hundred dollars was the amount offered for his misdemeanours in Laredo.

'Is he a friend of yours, or are you sadly in need of five hundred dollars?'

'He's no friend of mine. Let's say he's done my family harm at an earlier date. I don't suppose you've seen anything of him in the past few days, marshal?'

'Can't say I have, amigo, but now that you've drawn my notice to him I'll keep a sharp lookout in the future. Will you be stayin' around town?'

'I don't have any interest in the area, other than locatin' that fellow, Lopez. If I find him, I'll be in touch, of course. Adios, and thanks.'

Drifter replaced his hat and moved towards the door. At the same time, Fuente opened it and stepped indoors, his dark round eyes almost bulging with curiosity. Drifter side-stepped him and regained the sidewalk, where he stood beside the sorrel's head, knuckling it gently above the muzzle.

Once again, he watched the strollers who seemed especially interested in himself. Before he had made up his mind what to do, he was observed through the window by the Mexican deputy. Fuente's friendly expression had undergone a change, probably because he had seen Lopez's likeness and he did not like white Americans making money out of Mexican criminals.

Drifter winked at the deputy, feeling slightly amused by the latter's rather vicious expression. Presently, he mounted up and rode the sorrel towards the west end of town. The livery he decided to patronise was the last building on the north side. He dismounted, turned over the sorrel to a long, gangling youth who was shirtless in bibbed overalls and a straw hat.

'I'd like for you to give him a good groomin' and a light meal of oats. I don't rightly know whether I'll be in town overnight, but I'll sure enough contact you later. That be all right?'

The youth nodded, acknowledging the instructions, but said nothing. Out on the street again, Drifter sought the comparative shade of a sidewalk awning. He rolled a cigarette, stuck it in his mouth and lighted it before going off to combine business with pleasure.

There were three hotels in town. In one of them, known as the Border Settlement, he asked for a bath and a meal, but declined to book a room. An elderly attendant carried many buckets of water up to the bathroom for him and, later, indicated the direction of the dining room.

Early in the afternoon, the pull of the heat began to affect the tall young Texan. He fought off the desire to take a full siesta and compromised by dozing in the chair of a Mexican barber who delicately thinned out the thick auburn hair on his crown and round the sides and back of his head.

Declining to have his beard and sideburns trimmed, he indicated that he was ready to leave. He tipped generously and stooped slightly while the barber dusted off his neck and shoulders.

'Anything else I can do for you, señor?'

Drifter shook his head, grinned and then changed his mind. 'Well there is one little thing. If a man wanted to settle in this town, he'd feel secure if he knew there was a tidy little bank in which to put his savings. I'm sure you'd agree on that. Not that I have a lot of money. But I'd like to think it was safe. You look like you've been here all your life. Maybe you could suggest the right place for me to use?'

The Mexican chuckled. He deftly folded the towel which had been draped round his customer's neck. 'Marshal O'Halloran thinks that all our banks are safe. Probably, he is right. El Mestizo, our notorious border *bandido*, has never been seen in this town. They say he is mad for gold. Perhaps we don't have the gold to attract him here. But you are asking a serious question.

'We have two banks. The big building over on Second Street is a branch of the Central and South Western Bank. Most of the influential Texans use that one. The Rio and Laredo Bank at the east end of town is smaller. In fact, I don't think it has any real connection with Laredo, at all.

'All the same, its owner always looks prosperous. He welcomes the savings of Texans an' Mexicans alike, an' that is good. After all, money is money, is it not, señor? You must take your choice.'

Drifter so far unbent that he shook hands with the barber before going onto the street again. Once again, the heat between the buildings began to knock him. Sprawling sleeping bodies annoyed him as he stepped carefully along the boardwalks, studying the buildings with a professional eye.

There were four saloons altogether. Having sampled the beer in the Border earlier, he avoided that establishment but slaked his thirst in each of the others. As he drank, he studied the buildings round about him. He soon dismissed the towering stone-based branch of the Central and South Western Territories Bank as being beyond the scope of himself and his partner.

The Rio and Laredo Bank, by contrast, appeared to be just about right. It was a two storey building of brick and glass on the end of a block of shops and offices on the south side of the east end of Main Street.

Its front entrance was on Main. An alley separated it from the offices alongside of it. An open wooden staircase gave outside access to the upper storey from the alley itself. At the rear was another entrance, opening out into Third Street on the south side.

On other corners near at hand were a mail office, a saddler's shop and a millinery establishment. An ageing gaunt-faced man wearing a bush hat and a soiled apron rocked back and forth like a pendulum on the shaded sidewalk outside the saddler's. It was not at all clear whether he was generally interested in the infrequent comings and goings in the heat of the day, or more specifically in the plump milliner who for some reason had chosen that time to sweep the boards in front of her shop.

On a verandah outside the nearest

beer parlour, Drifter toyed with his glass until he felt that he had seen enough. He then rose to his feet, crossed the dirt of the street somewhat uncertainly and mounted the sidewalk opposite, treading like a sleep-walker.

He contrived to take notice of the details posted on the door of the bank concerning opening hours. He had a faraway look in his eyes as he rounded the building, observed by the rocking saddler, and went off in the opposite direction down Third. A half hour later, he had collected the sorrel and commenced his return journey.

For the first hour, the sorrel did all the work, finding its way with comparative ease, while Drifter dozed on its back and daydreamed about the cooling waters of the creek by the hideout.

Some time later, when they had left the well-marked trail and entered timber, the rider slowly became alert again. He began to wonder if Lopez had discovered his hiding place for the bottle of whiskey, a little of which had been used for medicinal purposes the night before.

Usually, his Texican cousin was predictable, but just occasionally he went against his usual habits and did something entirely out of character. Sometimes he would fish for hours and provide the wherewithal for a good meal. Other times, he would hunt, or carry out some irksome chores which neither of them wanted to do.

On this occasion, no sounds came from the direction of the shack as Drifter angled the tired sorrel through the trees in the last furlong. The unnatural quietness ought to have warned him that mischief was afoot, but on this occasion he did not react quickly enough. The loop which dropped out of the tree above him made no more sound than a bat.

Apart from having his hat brushed he had no warning until the rawhide gripped his upper arms and started to tighten. He flinched and instantly experienced apprehension and anger.

His spurs dug into the flanks of the sorrel before he tightened his leg grip on its barrel.

The startled animal leapt forward. The rider's leg grip held for a few seconds while the lariat tightened. Drifter was drawn backwards over the croup, but not before his weight and the horse's effort had dislodged the ambusher from his perch in the tree.

Lopez's gusty yell of triumph was cut short as his grip on the lariat caused him to lose his balance. In a matter of seconds, Drifter had landed heavily on his shoulders, losing his stetson in the process. When he contrived to turn around, he found Lopez two yards away, grinning ruefully and rubbing his head as he forced himself up to his knees.

'Land's sakes, cousin, what sort of a fool trick was that? Aren't you ever goin' to grow out of your childhood pranks? One of us might have been seriously hurt. Or I could have shot you, if I'd reacted quicker.'

'I guess it was something of a fool's trick at that,' Lopez conceded, when he recovered his breath. 'I thought maybe your trip to town had left you feelin' bored. The truth is, I wanted you to know I was on the alert while you were away. I reckon I'm sorry, if that makes you feel any better.'

Drifter muttered a few rounded oaths. He then used his strength to free himself of the loop. Without further ado, he stood up and walked off towards the creek. He had been swimming for five minutes when Lopez came up from the depths beside him.

In spite of his anger, the young Texan managed to grin.

4

Late that evening, the partners played cards over the wooden table before retiring. The time went by quickly enough. It was not until the lamp started to flicker that their concentration was broken and they entertained the idea of going to bed.

When Drifter declined to play another hand, Lopez started to yawn repeatedly. He rose tiredly to his feet and threw wood on the stove. Presently, his weariness communicated itself to Drifter, who preceded him up the ladder to the loft.

'You'll want me to make an early start,' Lopez called after him.

'Sure. First thing after breakfast. Get right on into town, don't hang around makin' yourself at home. The bank is easy to locate at the east end of Main Street. Do jest enough to make your presence known. Then clear out. Throw the pursuit and get back here unattended.'

Lopez made the ladder creak as he went up it with the lamp in his hand.

'I bet you get the shakes when you're waitin' for me to return, cousin,' he remarked knowingly.

'There could be a bit of the truth in that,' Drifter admitted. 'Waitin' an' not knowin' is kind of wearin' on the nerves. I reckon I age a little till I know you've made it away.'

Lopez leaned over him as he slithered into his bed and pulled the blanket around him.

'Why don't you ride in with me? You could get the drop on me shortly after I've hit the bank. That way it would be all over an' done with real soon.'

Drifter stared thoughtfully up into the rafters, where a spider was working late on a web. He kept Lopez waiting for a while before he gave a negative shake of the head.

'Nope. That wouldn't do.'

'Why not, for goodness' sake?'

'Because we don't want you caught straight away. We want to give the locals a chance to increase the price on your head! After all, we're only in this game for the money. Or had you forgotten?'

Lopez nodded, grunted and flopped back on his bed. 'Yer, that's right, cousin. As you say, we're only in it for the money. But you could ride into town an' make sure that I get clear. How would that be? Do you fancy a bit of excitement?'

'Excitement is better than waitin' an' not knowin'. I'll grant you that. On the other hand, there's always a chance some thinkin' townsman might figure out that we're in cahoots on the job, an' that could land us both in jail. I guess we'll have to do it like we've planned. I'll think of something to stop my nerves jumpin'.'

Drifter propped himself up on an elbow and studied his swarthy cousin's expression. 'You haven't been havin' one of those premonitions of yours, have you? You don't think this one is

49

goin' to be a bad strike?'

Lopez started to whistle, making a show of enforced gaiety.

'No, no, it isn't that. I'll be all right. It's jest that, well, it's nice to know you're not out there on your own. That there's a friendly pardner not far off, willin' you to pull off the job. Loneliness, that's all. And we won't discuss it further, otherwise we won't sleep well, an' that won't do.'

Drifter frowned, nodded and settled himself down again. The crackling of logs lulled them to sleep.

* * *

Lopez was ready to leave for town around eight the following morning. Drifter had prepared the breakfast and done everything to make sure that there was no delay to put back the plan. The Texan checked over the roan's saddle harness in a last minute attempt to make sure that nothing untoward could happen.

At last, Lopez was in the saddle. He delayed for a couple of minutes, laughing and playing around with the blue bandanna which he was supposed to use for a mask.

'Don't cover your features entirely, otherwise anyone seeing you won't tie you in with the reward notice.'

Lopez chuckled infectiously. 'I reckon I must be the only *bandido* in the border country who wants his identity to become known. Let's hope we amount to something one of these days. You'll be on the alert this afternoon, jest in case I haven't shaken the pursuit?'

Momentarily, Drifter looked troubled. With an effort, he shrugged aside his doubts. 'You'll have shaken them, all right,' he replied, reassuringly, 'but in any case I'll be on the alert. Like you were yesterday.'

Recollections of their earlier coming together helped to ease any late tension in Lopez. He managed to leave with a light heart, and Drifter was the one who felt like chewing his finger nails.

Around two in the afternoon, Drifter started to come up from the creek. In the forenoon, he had spent a lot of time cleaning the cabin. After that, he had rigged some low jumps and given the sorrel a bit of practice in going over them. Subsequently, he ran out of ideas for passing the time around the building and took himself off to the stream.

There, he bathed for upwards of an hour. When that activity began to grow wearisome, he left the water and dried himself in the sun. The fishing, which he undertook next, came almost as an afterthought.

Success with his line came slowly, and so it was that the first two hours of the afternoon had gone by when he strolled back with half a dozen small fish dangling from a yard of line. He was unprepared for visitors, and the two down-at-heel men in trail garb, who moved into the cabin area from the south set the nerves of his stomach jumping when they were still some distance away.

In view of what might be happening on the way from Rio City, casual visitors had no place in his scheme of things. He forced himself to appear casual, whistling to himself as he entered the cabin some distance ahead of them.

He dumped the fish on the table, hurriedly studied the newcomers through the open door and a window, and decided that he had never seen them before. He thought it was quite possible that they had learned of the cabin from someone at the Abello place, as he had. Every yard they came nearer confirmed that their faces had never crossed his line of vision.

No doubt he would learn whether Carmelita's casual visitors had sent them on to the cabin. Time would tell. He stepped out of doors, gave them a wave and brief shout of welcome and then re-entered the shack to co-ordinate his thoughts. He studied the riders cautiously through a corner of the window.

The man on the buckskin was the older of the two. Possibly he was nearing forty. He had small grey eyes in a lined sunburned face. A soiled dun stetson, dented at the front, perched loftily on a shock of wiry fair hair which had grey highlights in it. He was short, round-shouldered and running to a paunch — which put some strain on the front of the faded grey shirt above belt level.

The other fellow, riding easily on a big skewbald, was younger: perhaps thirty years of age. He had ginger hair and blue eyes. His flat-crowned black stetson hid a bald crown. A short thick bristling moustache made up for the sparseness of his brows and had the effect of making his short upper lip seem longer. His red and green squared shirt was topped by a black vest.

Both men wore a pair of six-guns and they looked quite capable of giving a good account of themselves with firearms.

They were dismounting some fifteen yards away when the young Texan moved to the door, hatless, and stroking his modest auburn beard.

'Howdy, gents? Come on in, why don't you? I reckon you could use a cup of coffee after your ride. My name is Drifter. I'll be glad to make your acquaintance as soon as you've freshened up a little.'

The man with the paunch was the first into the building. He walked with a limp, hat in one hand and holding his hip with the other. It occurred to Drifter that he might be exaggerating his limp and wanting to have his hand near a holster.

The redhead, who was several inches taller, followed him in with a curious stiff-backed way of walking. He sniffed the fish, grinned and nodded.

'My pardner's name is Graft, Limpy Graft. Me, I'm Red Marvin, We're jest ridin' through. On our way to no place in particular. Glad to know you, Drifter. It's almost as if you were expectin' company, what with all them small fishes an' all jest at the time of our arrival.'

'Take a seat at the table. I'll make some coffee,' Drifter offered. 'The best way to freshen yourselves is to go down the creek an' bathe, if you feel so minded.'

There was a brief hesitation between the two newcomers. 'Sure, Drifter,' Graft remarked, in a husky voice. 'I suppose we have to admit we're hungry, now that we see food about, an' a place to rest for a while.'

Drifter wanted them on their way with the absolute minimum of delay, but he knew he could not intimate such thoughts to them in so brief an acquaintance. He did not want to make them at all suspicious.

'I'll strip out your horses while you're bathin'. Take all the time you want.'

His suggestion again caused a short thoughtful silence. He knew they were wondering if he would go through their saddle pockets while they were down at the water's edge. Again, Graft was the one to accept the idea. Drifter went out ahead of them, and walked across to the cropping horses. He wondered what they were doing in the two minutes which elapsed before they came out and sauntered off down the slope.

While he was busily grooming their horses, he knew that they were really bathing. The shouting and the splashing easily carried to him. He denied himself the pleasure of rooting through their saddle pockets and made his way back to the cabin while they were still away.

The pot was bubbling. He gave a call and rapidly prepared the six fish for the frying pan. All the time he was busy, he was distracted by thoughts of Lopez, who was overdue. In their unusual line of business, no news most likely meant bad news.

Graft and Marvin returned together, except that one used the front door and the other, the rear. They did not intend

57

to be taken by surprise. However, the sizzling fish in the pan provided a surprise of sorts, and whatever conclusions they had come to about Drifter and the shack were buried while the eating was done.

Three o'clock saw the end of the meal. Marvin pushed aside the plates and mugs, while Graft rolled smokes for the three of them. Drifter accepted gratefully, sucking hard on the tobacco while his ears strained for sounds of an approaching horse. Marvin was the one to collect the playing cards from the sideboard and suggest a few hands to pass on the time.

Drifter found himself agreeing. The first two hands went his way. After that, Graft, who had been studying him ever since they met, asked a question which undermined the young Texan's morale.

'Tell me, Drifter, don't you find it lonely out here in the back of nowhere all by yourself?'

'A man can get used to almost anything, amigo,' he observed lightly. 'I thought all Texans were used to the wide open spaces an' their own company.'

Marvin put in a few comments as he shuffled the cards, but Drifter was slow to respond. His troubled thoughts had gone back to Lopez's absence. Probably his two unwanted guests already had seen the two beds in the loft. As likely as not, they had guessed that he was not entirely alone.

But where was Lopez?

The game restarted with Drifter playing automatically, and only managing to keep his thoughts in order with a great effort. The other two won a game apiece, and Graft was shaping up to win another when the sound of distant hooves carried into the building through the open back door.

All three of them flinched. Graft recovered first and continued his play. Marvin hesitated, and Drifter definitely threw in his hand.

'You two fellows are not expectin' further visitors, are you? I mean, I don't mind offerin' you hospitality, but if you have a group of riders followin' you up I don't have any big stock of provisions.'

'We don't have riders followin' us up,' Graft replied authoritatively.

'We hope, amigo,' Marvin added. 'Jest a few moments ago, I distinctly had the feelin' that *you* were expectin' someone. Maybe we ought to take a look-see who it is. Me an' my pardner, we don't always take kindly to surprises.'

Suddenly the game was a thing of the past. All three pushed back their bench seats and rose to their feet, crowding the back door and the window on that side. Drifter used his spyglass, training it hurriedly on a swelling group of riders entering the valley from the north side. Marvin drummed on his shoulder, anxious to take a look himself, while Graft worked his blunt teeth on the remains of an ancient plug of tobacco.

'Doggone it, hurry up, will you,

young fellow?' the lame man complained. 'They're makin' enough noise back there to rouse the dead. It ain't El Mestizo, the bandit, is it — '

'No it isn't.' Drifter confirmed hurriedly. 'Nothin' like that. I'd say it was an official posse, out from one of the nearby towns. I can see a star pinned to a man's shirt. Something big has happened, that's for sure, and they're comin' this way.'

Drifter surrendered the glass to Marvin, who muttered to himself about knowing where to focus it. In a matter of a few seconds, the group of riders had dispersed.

'What in tarnation are they doin', Red? Are you goin' to keep me in suspense all day?'

'Shucks, Limpy, they're makin' a tight ring round this shack, almost as if they had a wanted killer right here within their grasp!'

Drifter gasped. Graft wrested the glass from his partner and soon confirmed what was happening. He murmured: 'Ain't nobody in leather known to me. Of course, I can't speak for our new friend, here. He'd have to answer for himself.'

'That fellow with the big jaw is Marshal O'Halloran of Rio City,' Drifter explained. 'I met him jest a short while ago, though why he should come tearin' into these parts with a big posse I don't understand. As sure as fate he'll come askin' a lot of questions. If it's all the same to you, I'd like to do most of the answerin'. That all right?'

Drifter waited long enough for his visitors to nod in the affirmative. Almost at once he stepped out of doors with his Winchester to hand, looking as though he was outraged by the steadily closing ring of hostile riders.

'That you, Marshal O'Halloran? What in the world is goin' on? Do you have to search this neck of the woods with a posse big enough to defend the Alamo?'

The young Texan lowered his gun. His mouth had dried out as he was talking, but he hoped his underlying nervousness was not showing too obviously. All he could think of was that Lopez had shot up half the town and was due for lynching on sight.

About fifteen riders, in all, formed the tight ring round the cabin. The marshal came straight for the young Texan as soon as he heard his name called. Two others broke out and approached at the same time. One was Carlos Fuente, the Mexican deputy, and the other man was a stranger, a person of some standing in Rio by his clothes and bearing.

Fuente said: 'Caramba, it is the man who called about the reward notices! The very same one who was looking for Lopez! What a coincidence!'

He pronounced the word 'coincidence' carefully and with success, although it was newly in his vocabulary.

The third man urged his big grey gelding between the marshal's black and the deputy's pinto. 'What was that, Marshal? Did I hear correctly? This man actually came to town lookin' for the man we're seekin'?'

Looking slightly disgruntled, O'Halloran nodded vigorously and at the same time held up his hand to stem the other man's questions.

'All right, you men,' he shouted, 'cover every bit of ground, every tree in the area an' both banks of the stream. Then come back here!'

While the peace officer was giving out his orders, Drifter studied the gelding's rider and made an effort to get his nerves under control.

The man in the saddle looked lean and fit for his fifty years. A large cream-coloured stetson hid the fact that his crown was shaved entirely the way over. The only hair visible on his head occurred in his eyelids and brows. It was fair. His eroded green eyes were widely set apart in a full face dominated by a Roman nose. He wore a black tailored jacket over a white shirt and string tie, and a buttoned grey waistcoat. His trousers matched the waistcoat in colour.

A single Colt with pearl butt plates occupied a soft pigskin holster at his right hip. The line of his jaw was bedewed with perspiration.

O'Halloran dismounted carefully. He sent Fuente to check on the two men hovering round the doorway, and himself thrust his rifle back in the saddle scabbard.

'Yes, yes, yes, Mr Denver, this man did call at my office this week and asked about reward notices. The only one he showed any interest in was the one sent along from Laredo. Almost certainly, the man we are seekin' was the same fellow. I suppose you haven't seen Lopez anywhere around today?'

Drifter shook his head. 'Are you sayin' he's turned up in Rio? That he's done another armed robbery?'

O'Halloran nodded. He moved away a few feet, learned from Fuente that there was no sign of Lopez anywhere around, and came back to resume his conversation.

'What did you say your name was, friend?'

'I don't believe I mentioned it at our last meetin', but folks normally call me Drifter.'

'That ain't on your birth certificate, an' you know it!' the marshal snarled.

He was about to say more when the man in the cream stetson, who had dismounted, caught him by the arm. He checked his outburst.

'All right, all right. Drifter will do for now. This here is Mr. Denver, president of the Rio and Laredo Bank in town. He'd no doubt like to talk to you.'

Surprisingly, the banker advanced his hand and shook that of Drifter. 'Am I to take it that you know something of this man, Lopez, and his habits?'

Drifter gave a guarded answer, repeating that Lopez had given offence to his family before the time of the Laredo hold-up. He went on: 'I am not a bounty hunter by inclination, but I certainly would like to claim five hundred dollars for this man Lopez's hide!'

All the time he was talking a devious part of his mind was wondering what would happen if Lopez rode into the valley half-drunk with whiskey while they were still there. Drifter's hat seemed to tighten as unbidden perspiration beaded his brow.

Denver drew him aside, strolling with him along the front of the cabin. 'Drifter, I want this Lopez caught more than anything else in the world! In Laredo he pistol-whipped one man, an' shot another in the leg. Now, he strikes at my bank in Rio. My chief teller was struck over the head with a gun as he entered my private office, a place where I normally am at that time of the day.

'I might add that the teller in question could have choked to death with a cloth stuffed in his mouth if the clumsy bandit had not stumbled and made a lot of noise on his way out of the back door.'

'I hate to have to ask this, Mr Denver, but did he get away with a lot of the bank's money?'

Denver halted, his fists clenched and a lot of colour showing in his cheeks. Graft and Marvin, who were very interested in the latest goings on, managed to get within earshot quite unobserved by the angry banker.

'Indeed, he did. Money, valuables, belonging to the bank's best customers. My bank does business far in excess of its size, Drifter. Right now, I have a feelin' that Lopez has given the marshal's posse the slip. I'll tell you what I'll do. If you'll go after this character on my behalf I'll double the reward money already on offer!'

Drifter whistled. One part of his plan was paying off, even if their efforts were still fraught with danger. 'You mean you'll pay a thousand dollars for him, dead or alive, sir?'

'A thousand dollars, yes. But I want him alive. That has to be understood.'

Drifter was already nodding affirmatively as he led the way indoors.

5

During all the time since he had teamed up with Lopez, Drifter had never been so puzzled. This was a situation to tax the brain of some learned professor, or an international player of chess, not a drifting westerner.

Banker Denver, Marshal O'Halloran and the rest stayed for perhaps another half hour before mounting up again and leaving the valley in a south-westerly direction. Drifter went to the edge of the nearest clump of trees with them, raised his hat and waved, and then returned to the cabin.

His temporary visitors, Graft and Marvin, found him withdrawn into himself, busy with thoughts that would not sort themselves out into a reasonable pattern.

All he could think of was that Lopez was overdue: considerably so. That a sizeable posse was searching for him, and that his 'price' had been doubled. Most significant of all was the fact that Denver, the banker, wanted him alive. That seemed to suggest that Lopez had laid his hands on booty of some great value. Booty which had to be recovered before he was eliminated. Lopez would be made to tell where he had hidden it, if he was ever taken into custody.

Drifter wondered what the chances were of other people getting to Lopez before he did. After all, his Texican cousin had not returned to the cabin, their base. He might have had to stay away because the posse had headed him off, or he might just conceivably have decided to pull out alone with his special haul.

The more Drifter thought, the more he was puzzled about what to do for the future.

'When are you thinkin' of ridin' after that Lopez hombre, Drifter?' Graft queried, as they squatted on the grass at the shady side of the cabin.

'I haven't made up my mind about anything yet, Limpy. Why do you ask? What are your plans?'

Graft chuckled, shaking his paunch. Marvin explained: 'Well, we was thinkin' of movin' on when you do. Thought we might give you a hand with Lopez. If he's as much a menace as the marshal an' the banker made out, you could do with a couple of extra guns to tame him with.

'What do you say? Would you be prepared to share the thousand dollars three ways?'

Drifter shrugged. 'You don't have to wait for me. Why don't the pair of you go lookin' for him? If you take him in you could share the reward an' have five hundred apiece. I am sure Denver's offer would apply to anyone else.'

The other two were slow in answering, although their minds were made up. 'You're the one who's seen him before,' Graft murmured. 'You know his ways better than other folks. When you leave, we all leave.'

71

'I'll give it some thought,' Drifter promised.

He rose to his feet and strolled away, walking as far as the spot where the sorrel was pegged out. He did not want this pair of leeches along with him. They would cramp his style. At the same time, he could not afford to leave them in the cabin when he left to search for Lopez, on account of Lopez possibly getting back to the hideout and being jumped by them in his — Drifter's — absence.

So they had to go with him, and he had to get rid of them in some way or another before he started on the serious business of searching. Having come to that conclusion, he returned to the shack, followed the other two indoors and told them of his decision.

'We move out in a half hour. About four hours of daylight in hand. I plan to make for high ground, for a quick survey in all directions. That is, provided we don't see obvious signs of the fugitive before we get there.'

Graft and Marvin exchanged significant glances and seemed satisfied with the arrangement. All the time until they were mounted up and riding out of the clearing and valley, Drifter's nerves were on edge. He was really scared that Lopez would come riding directly into them and that he would have to make him a prisoner while the two strangers were around.

If the worst came to the worst, he supposed that he could take Lopez along to Rio City with the unwanted pair of hangers-on, and some time later arrange his escape, but at this time he felt that he had to have the chance to talk to Lopez in private.

Lopez, however, was nowhere near the hideout shack at that time. As the miles stretched out under the three horses, Drifter was able to relax more. Lopez was no fool, and out in the open it was unlikely that he would blunder into a trio of riders off the beaten track.

The young Texan's landmark objective was an east-west ridge a few miles to the north-west of the hideout. In average terrain, they should have covered the distance with an hour to spare before sundown, but over this route the going was rough and heavy, liberally cut up by eroded trail rocks and further rendered difficult by a series of low switchbacks which had the horses blowing hard and the riders cursing.

Consequently, the setting sun was well down beyond the peaks of the Sierra Madre mountains to westward and twilight was gathering in strength as the grumbling pair of trail partners toiled up the tortuous spine of the ridge from the eastern tip in Drifter's wake.

For over an hour, he had racked his brains for a way in which to give his companions the slip, but no scheme had come to mind. They had stayed close to him and — if anything — observed everything he did with too much attention for his comfort. It was almost as though they could read his thoughts.

Drifter dismounted and punished his legs in an effort to get ahead of the others. His personal effort began to pay off. When he was fifty yards ahead of them Graft called to him.

'Hey, Drifter, will you ease up a bit? This here cayuse under me is goin' to blow itself out before we get to the top of this God-forsaken heap of rock!'

Drifter looked back and waved placatingly. Ahead of him and to his left was a sub-track; one which he had seen before in his travels. He extracted his spyglass from a saddle pocket, and sent the sorrel into the sidetrack, spanking its rump to keep it moving.

'Why don't you hole up right where you are, Limpy? Me, I'm goin' on jest a little bit further to get a good vantage point to look around from.'

There was a lot of muttering from the other two, who had suffered considerable discomfort in the pro-tracted ride. They glowered at him. Marvin pointed, too, but apparently they were satisfied to bed down without looking around that night themselves. After all, they had achieved their main object, that of keeping in touch with Drifter, the key to future profit.

Twenty yards further on, Drifter went out of sight behind some tenuous green prickly bushes. When his actions were further screened by moss and ferns he began to deliberately slide down the slope on the south side, which was to his left. He was directly above a continuation of the track onto which he had pushed the sorrel and heading straight for it in a slightly precipitous manner.

After dropping some ten or fifteen yards, he lost his footing but a very spiky plant caught in his shirt and helped to decelerate his progress. He straightened up on the narrow track itself and at once gave the sharp protracted whistle with which he always summoned his mount from a distance.

He aimed his whistle uphill to try and fool his companions. The sorrel reacted at once. Two minutes later, it was beside him. He mounted up, sent it forward and quickly found a downward leading track angled to about forty-five degrees with the horizontal.

Graft started to shout after him when he was half way down it, but he paid no attention. By the time the other two found out where he was, no more than fifty feet of slope remained to be negotiated to the valley floor and pursuit was out of the question in the fading light.

★ ★ ★

Even with a useful moon to assist, the return journey to the hideout cabin by night was a stamina sapping effort with a lot of minor hazards involved. Drifter used to the full the faculties of the sorrel and from time to time he dismounted and rocked the saddle to afford it some slight relief. Luck was with him: even so, the hour was past two in the morning when the flagging animal carried him into the valley. Lopez had not returned. No one else had visited the place. The stove was out. Only an owl and a distant coyote betokened any sort of life at all.

Drifter hauled off the saddle harness, picked up his weapons and climbed to the loft where he flopped out almost at once and slept until dawn.

★ ★ ★

Some four hours later, when dawn was still a tentative affair, he roused himself, built a small fire in the stove and made a light breakfast of coffee and biscuits. No one had approached the spot in the night. Everything was as it had been when he left the previous day.

He scribbled a note for Lopez and pinned it on the underside of his bed. It suggested that Drifter was out looking for him, and that he intended to be back in about two days.

By the time he rode out of the valley towards the east, primed by a rough local map, he was frowning at the enormity of his task, and wondering if he and his partner had parted for the last time. Frequently, he had thought of parting company with Lopez, but this was not the way. He had to find out what had happened to his reckless cousin.

Even if Lopez had headed for the Mexican border, his mind and attitude changed by the sight of much loot, Drifter felt that he had to know the truth before he stopped searching and made other plans.

Two hours after he started out, his rough track converged with the main trail running south from Rio City towards the Rio Grande river, which formed the boundary between the United States and Mexico. He started to encounter travellers, although the traffic was thin on the north-south route. Three enquiries before noon failed to produce any knowledge of Lopez or anyone answering his description.

Some time later, when he was long overdue for a rest and keen for a bit of human company he came upon a covered wagon off-trail on the east side. The family in charge of it had pulled off the trail for their midday meal and, as there was a slight down gradient on that side of the track, the shaft horses were finding it hard to pull the wagon clear again.

Drifter reined in, touched his hat and looked them over.

The man at the head of the team, a rotund Mexican in his early fifties, stopped struggling with the horses. He flapped his bolero, removed his steeple hat and mopped his brow. His ample jowl and lush brown moustache were also groomed with a cloth before he was satisfied.

'Buenos dias, señor, you find us at a difficult time.'

Drifter dismounted and returned the greeting. His attention was on the other members of the party. Up on the box was the wife, a stern-looking woman in a black skirt and blouse. Her brown eyes twinkled as a smile softened the lines of her face. Her left hand went to her generous bosom, as though she was wondering about her appearance. She slumped back on the seat.

Looking very attractive beside the vehicle was a young woman in her early twenties. She was sitting side-saddle on a bare-backed brown mare. She had a long neck and sloping shoulders. Her shapely figure looked good in a white peasant blouse and a short riding skirt. Her long bare legs ended in white half boots which made them seem even longer. She tossed back a fine head of hair the colour of burnished copper and favoured Drifter with a fetching smile which sat easily on her full lips. Eyes which were almost violet in colour intrigued the young Texan and made him want to know her better.

Without being aware of it, he had been staring at her. His attention was distracted quite soon, however, when a fourth person came around from the tailgate where he had been pushing and halted beside the riding horse with his hands on his hips.

This was a man of slightly over average height with a compact, muscular body and a pair of intense blue eyes which gave the impression that he could see right into a man's soul. Drifter supposed that he was in his thirties. He was clean-shaven, with plenty of fair hair on his head, hidden under a low flat Quaker-style hat. His white shirt was open at the neck. His black trousers looked as though they were part of a suit.

He said. 'Good day to you, friend. We are in need of someone who can work a minor miracle to get us back on the trail. Do you think you could help us?'

'I sure would like to try, sir,' Drifter replied. He walked forward and shook hands with the blue-eyed man. 'My name is Drifter. At your service.'

'Glad to meet you, Mr. Drifter. Meet Cipriana. Over there, her mother,

Señora Carreras, and behind you, Señor Carreras, the owner of the wagon. I'm Joseph. I travel with them.'

Drifter nodded and smiled to each of them. He was conscious of a blush under his tan long after his eyes had left those of the girl. With an effort, he turned his mind to the current problem. After walking round the wagon and examining the state of the wheels and the dirt surface under them, he had a suggestion to make.

'It seems to me that if we dug out some of this soft earth from in front of the rear wheels an' maybe improved the surface with a few small rocks an' branches the wagon would roll forward a lot easier.'

Joseph accepted the idea at once. He collected a spade from the rear and only surrendered it into Drifter's hands when the latter insisted. Perspiration showed as the digging got under way. Cipriana took charge of his hat, while the older couple looked on anxiously and wondered if the plan would work.

Presently, while Drifter was leaning against the canvas and accepting a drink of water, Joseph came back with an armful of small branches and the necessary stones. Five minutes later they were ready to make the attempt. Ernesto, the father, mounted up on the box. Drifter took the lead horses by the head harness, and the others moved round to the tailgate to push.

Drifter's American words of encouragement mingled with Ernesto's Spanish inducements. The horses made a few feet of progress before the stones and branches ceased to have an effect. A second great effort, however, had the desired result. The big heavy wagon lurched onto the trail proper and turned to go towards the south.

Ernesto slammed on the brakes and joined the others who were swarming round Drifter to thank him. The warmth of Mexicans' gratitude was almost overwhelming for a time. Alicia, the wife, very soon found out that he had eaten little that day. A big pot, in which was some warm stew, was hoisted out of the vehicle, along with other items to make a scratch meal. Cipriana saw to his requirements as he squatted on a flat trail-side rock and replenished his empty stomach. For a time, during which the girl delicately fussed him till he felt like a king, Lopez was out of his thoughts.

The party was anxious to make tracks for the south, but no one rushed him into hurrying his meal. At length, Joseph came and sat beside him, giving him an opportunity to talk about himself, if he so wanted.

'Thanks for a fine meal, you good people. I have one favour to ask, which may have a bearing on my future movements. I'm lookin' for a friend.'

He went on to describe Lopez, dwelling on his physical appearance, his little mannerisms and the type of horse he was riding. When he raised his eyes he was surprised to see them all smiling at him.

Joseph considerately satisfied his curiosity.

'Such a man spent last night in camp with us. He seemed restless and unsure of himself, but we made him welcome. He ate with us and slept around our fire. He snored, in fact. Only this morning he was awake very early. He did not want to wait even for breakfast. He borrowed a razor and one or two other things, and hurriedly made tracks for the north.'

'For the *north*?' Drifter repeated, as though puzzled.

'Si, señor,' Ernesto put in. 'He rode up this same track towards the north. There is no doubt about the direction which he took.'

Drifter nodded, smiled and accepted what they had told him. Clearly they were intrigued by Lopez and would have liked to know more about his affairs and the link between the two of them. He felt they were owed some slight explanation. He forced himself to give up speculating as to whether Lopez would double back south again, or head for the valley hideout.

Something in Joseph's blue eyes made him say more than he would have done to almost any other casual acquaintance.

'By his appearance, you would find it hard to believe that your other visitor is my cousin. Mostly, we move around together. But he gets restless at times, and unsure of himself. I must go after him, if you will now excuse me for rushin' away.'

Drifter shook hands with Ernesto and Alicia. Without realising what he was going to do, he kissed the hand of the girl, Cipriana, and finally gripped the powerful hand of Joseph, who afterwards insisted upon boosting him into the saddle.

Drifter lifted his hat to a chorus of farewells. He sent the sorrel off up the track towards the north. From time to time, he glanced back at the girl who continued to wave.

The powerful cultured voice of

Joseph called after him something that sounded like 'Vaya usted con dio' and then they were out of earshot, and suddenly out of sight because of a bend.

6

For upwards of half an hour after the wagoners had been hidden from view, Drifter's thoughts were still on them. The girl's lissom beauty had had a profound effect upon him. He kept seeing her over and over again in his mind's eye as she had first appeared to him seated bareback on the brown mare. There was something about those violet eyes, and the remarkable sheen on her hair. Hers was definitely copper-coloured. His own hair, auburn with a few reddish highlights, looked almost mousy by comparison.

He said: 'She had no rings upon her fingers,' and then wondered what had prompted him to say such a thing.

Presently, his thoughts came back to his self-imposed task; that of searching for Lopez. Cipriana was a fine girl and, evidently unattached, but she was not for the likes of him, an ordinary drifter with little talent for making a living. For him was a homely unreliable half-breed cousin. Lopez.

A man riding on a buckboard who might have been a preacher or a doctor jogged by, but the fellow was withdrawn into himself and scarcely in a frame of mind to pass the time of day with a strange rider.

Accordingly, Drifter merely touched his hat and carried on going.

At the end of an hour, the sorrel began to tire again: with the animal's weariness, the rider began to feel impatient. Why was Lopez heading north again? Was he heading north, or had he hoodwinked those who had helped him by setting off in that direction? Clearly any protracted ride north would put the fellow a long way from the hideout shack where they were supposed to meet.

The track was a dusty eroded one, much given to winding in and out. At no time was the solitary rider able to see very far in front of him. Consequently, to appease his frustration and at the same time give the sorrel a breather, he looked for a suitable observation point on high ground.

A half mile further on, he observed a giant rocky outcrop. It resembled a huge finger of stone jutting up out of the earth and crooked half way up, at a height of perhaps thirty feet. Earth and talus supported it on the north side to which it was apparently leaning.

He decided to scramble up to the top of it with his spyglass and make use of the view from the top. Ten minutes later, he turned his mount off-trail, dismounted and loosened the saddle, which he rocked. Slapping the animal on the rump, he drove it further away from the trailside rock to forage for grass.

Just before he attempted the climb, he blinked hard, grumbled to himself about forgetfulness, and went after the beast. From the saddle pockets he took a pair of mocassins and the glass, which he had forgotten. He was breathless before he had made half the ascent. By resting twice and doing some deep-breathing each time, he eventually reached the top and threw himself down in a moss-covered cavity.

For a time, his eyes swam with perspiration. He licked salt off his upper lip, and made a thorough job of wiping out his stetson before he attempted to look around. As soon as he glanced towards the north, he met with a surprise. A solitary rider on a dark horse was slowly plodding south-wards.

His questing mind at once pegged the newcomer for Lopez, but he shook his head and decided it was wishful thinking. There was no earthly reason why his cousin should be coming towards him, actually moving south again, at that particular time. He was slow to put the glass to his eye, but when he did he had all the confirmation he needed. It *was* Lopez. There was no doubt about it. He was hunched in the saddle as though tired of riding with his steeple hat bumping lightly against his shoulder blades, supported by its cord.

Drifter frowned, clenched his teeth and finally began to smile. Whatever Lopez had done, whatever he was planning to do in the future, a lot of Drifter's uncertainty about what lay ahead of them in the future was about to be clarified.

The descent was slightly more perilous than the ascent, but the climber's mood had changed. Long before he reached the bottom, he had made up his mind to go forward a little up the trail and to find a suitable spot for a mock ambush. The sorrel proved elusive when he wanted to grab it and tighten up the cinches, but he spoke sharply to it and presently he had forked the saddle and moved back onto the trail proper.

About one hundred and fifty yards on, he found the right sort of rock cover for his 'ambush'. The trailside rocks over a distance of some seventy yards were arranged by nature so that they started small, went gradually bigger in size to the middle and then slowly grew smaller again until they were less than three feet high. Moreover, they were in depth, and just about the middle — like a gap in a set of teeth — there was a narrow defile going away from the trail for between forty and fifty feet.

As he reached the gap, Drifter reined in, stared at the distant slumped figure lolling round the roan's neck while his own mount turned tentatively in a circle, and then moved out of sight. No doubt at this stage the sorrel was wondering whether this was going to be another abortive rest period. It was disappointed. The screening rocks on either side towered to twelve feet, topping the head of a mounted rider. Drifter contented himself with turning the beast about to face the trail. He leisurely removed his Winchester from the scabbard and cradled it across the saddle.

He was thirsty and he felt like a

drink, but it could wait until he had given Lopez one of the surprises of his relatively short life.

★ ★ ★

No sooner was the sorrel and its master hidden from view than Lopez straightened up. He was cautious enough to keep the roan moving at the same speed, having spotted his partner and noticed his point of departure from the trail. He, too was grinning. He was seeing himself in the role of ambushing an ambusher. Drifter's profile was so familiar to him that he had not needed any artificial aid to the eyesight.

He started to make calculations, using energy which he had begun to think had totally gone back upon him. His wits were clear. He checked out his plan and saw that it should work. As soon as the vital line of rocks started to go by, he eased the roan closer to them, carefully removed his feet from the stirrups and unfastened his spurs.

Hooking them round his saddle horn, he then waited for a rock of a suitable height to go by and launched himself onto the top of it, risking losing fragments of skin and the possibility of acquiring a few bruises.

He landed reasonably well and silently, almost: a fiendish face, accompanied by aggressive arm gestures assured that the roan went on for a few paces more. Lopez then turned his attention to crossing the tops of the rocks and, in about half a minute, he pulled up short not more than a yard or two from his silent companion.

Both of them heard the roan slow down to a stop, short of the gap at the trailside. With just the top of his head over the rock edge, Lopez witnessed the changing expression on Drifter's face. While the ambusher was still undecided what to do next, Lopez clicked back the hammer of a revolver and aimed it down at the side of his head.

'Hey, hey, amigo, how's that for a surprise?'

Drifter stiffened. The sorrel shifted under him, and presently he inclined his head in the direction of the pointing weapon. One of Lopez's beady brown eyes was lined up right behind the gun, and his gapped-tooth grin fanned out on either side.

'All right, so you weren't asleep in the saddle, but you've been a devil of a long time gettin' in touch with me since the strike in town, an' what's more you weren't headin' in the right direction to find me!'

Lopez chuckled. 'Right now is not the time for recriminations, cousin. I haven't yet decided whether or not to put a bullet through that fine headgear of yours. I reckon it would give me a whole lot of pleasure jest to do that.'

'All the time you are hunkered down on that rock, you are lessenin' your chances of stayin' out of jail. Get down off there while you are still unobserved!'

Lopez's expression grew more menacing, as though he would have liked to put a whole lot more pressure upon his cousin. The gun remained in position for a few seconds longer, but the eyes behind it withdrew and took a cursory look around, up and down trail. In the meantime, Drifter backed his sorrel still further away from the track. As soon as he had sufficient room in which to turn round, he did so.

Some fifty yards further off-trail there was a small natural park of about twenty square yards bordered by waist-high rocks. It provided a good temporary stopping place for men who had much to say to each other. Lopez joined him almost at once. They stripped off their saddles, roughly groomed their horses and built a low fire.

Before the coffee pot came to the boil, Drifter started to ask his questions. 'We've been together for quite a time now, cousin, so, after what's happened I'd be obliged if you'd give me a few straight answers. I have to admit that what you've been doin' baffles me.

'First off, I reckon you ran out on me. Now, try an' make me believe otherwise!'

Lopez hunkered down in front of a rock. He spread his hands, palm upwards. 'Cousin, the only reason I didn't come straight to the cabin was because the father and mother of a posse got between me an' the way I wanted to go. You should have seen them!'

'I did see them. They came to the hideout shack where I was waitin' for you. That much I could believe, if I hadn't jest found you riding the wrong way. Now, where's the loot you picked up from the bank?'

The Texican, whose mobile expression had begun to show confidence, abruptly looked nonplussed. He fingered his black stubbled chin with squarely-cut finger nails. Shortly after a shave he always looked as if he was ready for another.

'Cousin, you have to believe me, this was no ordinary pick-up. It was worth a king's ransom. It is temporarily out of my possession, right now. I had to hide it, an' that's the truth!'

In a sudden outburst of temper, Drifter hurled a small stone into the fire, dislodging a few burning twigs and sending up a shower of sparks. When the coffee pot almost capsized, he rose to his feet and poured for himself, turning his back upon his partner. When Lopez had also taken a mug of coffee, and mildly scalded his lips, Drifter resumed.

'Hell an' tarnation, cousin, you've bungled the job an' you won't admit it! I reckon you nearly left a bank employee to suffocate, an' you came away with nothin'. Now ain't that the truth?'

'No, no, no, it ain't the truth!' In his emotional state, Lopez slopped coffee over his finger and hurriedly transferred his mug to the other hand. 'I *did* get the loot. I stashed it away on a covered wagon belongin' to a family I met further down the trail!'

'Liar!' Drifter bellowed. 'I met the same family, an' I stayed with them for maybe an hour or more. They admitted to knowin' you, but they didn't say anythin' about you leavin' anything with them.'

Lopez rose to his feet, rumbling angrily deep in his throat. He spat into the fire, and followed up by hurling the last half inch of his coffee into it.

'Cousin, you've got it all wrong! You're too darned suspicious this trip to listen! I was on my way back to collect when you spotted me a few minutes ago!'

A couple of yards apart, they stood facing each other, both extremely tense and consumed by anger.

'Cousin, I'm fresh out of believin' you, an' that's a fact. I can tell you that the reward money on your head has been doubled! The bank president is offerin' one thousand dollars cash, provided you're taken in alive! An' that's where you're goin', back to Rio City like we planned!'

Lopez thought over the new revelation, but it did nothing to appease his anger. He pointed a hairy index finger at Drifter's chest.

'But even a thousand dollars is chicken feed to what I picked up in the town! This is a time for changin' the plans! Can't you see what I'm gettin' at?'

Drifter nodded, and then suddenly swung at him. Thumped alongside of the jaw, Lopez staggered sideways. Due to the unevenness of the ground, Drifter was wide with his follow-up punches. Lopez caught him sharply twice, above the belt. The fight developed in ferocity. One of Lopez's nostrils leaked blood. Drifter's mouth was cut.

'All right, boys, that'll be jest about enough!'

The two fighters sprang back and faced about. On either side of the high rocks which flanked the short narrow passage, a man was lying prone with a rifle trained on them. To Lopez they

102

were total strangers, but Drifter knew them well enough. Limpy Graft and Red Marvin, the two men in the district he least wanted to see.

7

Within five minutes of the sudden occurrence, Drifter and Lopez were sitting with their backs to rocks with their wrists and ankles securely tied with hogging strings. Neither of them had anything to say. They were feeling downcast and angry with themselves for allowing a couple of strangers to take them unawares with such ease.

The coffee pot had been topped up again and the two newcomers were partaking of a light meal before moving on again to a destination of their choosing.

Lopez had proved more of a curiosity to both of them than Drifter, due to the former's reputation put around by the banker and the marshal. The prisoners would have better suited their captors' purpose if they had talked and revealed things about themselves.

Clearly, the interlopers had heard a few of the exchanges between their prisoners before they had intimated their presence.

After a short interval, Graft had things to say. 'Mercy me, if you two ain't a pair of the shiftiest characters it's ever been my misfortune to meet. What do you say, Red?'

'Wouldn't surprise me if they both told far more lies than truth, Limpy. Anyways, that hombre with the swarthy skin will come up against one or two experts back in Rio when they want a few questions answered.'

Lopez cleared his throat. 'You figurin' on takin' the two of us into Rio City, amigo?'

'That's about the size of things,' Graft confirmed. 'There was a time when we were real friendly with that buddy of yours, but since he gave us the slip when we'd agreed to be his pardners, we don't like him any more. Maybe if we took him in at the same time as you, the banker an' the marshal could pin some sort of a reward on him for not bringing you in promptly, like he was supposed to do.'

'We promised to split three ways,' Drifter reminded them, although he did not expect them to take much notice of him.

'That was before you lit out on the side of that ridge,' Marvin retorted.

'How do you know I wouldn't have come back lookin' for you after I'd tracked him down? Believe me, he's real mean when he's cornered, either one of you could have been shot dead. In leavin' you when I did, I could have been doin' you a real big favour.'

Marvin at first looked as if he felt like working Drifter over with his fists, but Graft's grinning face made him think better of the idea, and presently they broke camp. The prisoners' ankles were untied so that they could mount up, but their wrists remained secured, and their weapons were all removed.

Marvin took the lead as they

emerged on the trail, controlling Drifter's mount by holding the reins. Lopez was similarly placed alongside of Graft.

'Gents,' Lopez pleaded, 'If you'd listen to me I could put more than a thousand dollars into your eager hands, an' that's a fact!'

Graft shook his head. 'Me an' my buddy, we're gamblers, all right. We like easy money. But that thousand dollars, promised by the banker is a dead cert, the way we figure it out. Certain pay dirt. So save your breath, Señor Lopez. You couldn't convince your own pardner, so don't try out words on us.'

The quartet moved northwards for a good three hours, covering more than half of the journey towards their destination. When nearly ten miles had gone by and dust and thirst were dogging the outfit, Graft began to look around for a night camping spot.

Drifter indicated one or two places which he thought were suitable, but his suggestions were given short shrift and so he kept his peace. Their attitude showed that they were still very hostile towards him. Perhaps a night's rest might improve his future. He was pleased that the traffic in the other direction had been thin.

Their captors had shown not the slightest interest in other wayfarers, and the southbound travellers had taken the hint and refrained from asking probing questions.

Presently, on the west side of the trail, Marvin located a pool of still water. Drifter did not like the look of it, but Graft's buckskin took a tentative drink and appeared to approve of the liquid, and that was all the confirmation the tired limping man required.

The captors did all the work connected with fire building and tending the horses. The prisoners had to be content with a few minutes of exercise after the meal, before their ankles were trussed for the night.

The sun was slow to go down. Drifter fretted over his ankle bonds which Marvin had tied tighter than was really necessary. Lopez, by contrast, had more trouble with his wrist bonds. As the gathering gloom closed in upon them, Graft made it clear that he was going to keep awake for the first two hours.

Having come so close to a thousand dollars reward, the captors were not going to let it slip through carelessness in the night.

Red Marvin was slow to settle. He thought about trimming his spiky moustache and then decided against it. His bedding-down spot did not suit him. He tried laying his head against his saddle but that was not comfortable enough. Next, he took off his stetson and pushed the side of his face into it.

Lopez, who was nearest to him, blinked his cunning eyes and planned a little mischief.

'Say, amigo, what does Marvin's bald head, shinin' in the firelight remind you of? Don't think about it. Jest blurt out the first thing that comes into your mind.'

Drifter yawned. 'Well, I don't rightly

know at this late hour, pardner. I'd say he looks as if he'd been scalped at a very tender age. Wouldn't you?'

Marvin sat up suddenly. He looked as if he would have risen to his feet and attacked the two prisoners. Two things stopped him. He did not like to go into action without his boots on, and Graft was looking almost as pleased as the prisoners.

'All right, Drifter,' Marvin muttered. 'Ease off with the wisecracks, unless you want me to come over there an' lift your scalp! It wouldn't take me long. Then your buddy could make up his mind which of us is the prettier!'

Both prisoners shook with laughter. Graft chewed solidly on his chaw of tobacco. Presently, Drifter started to whistle to himself, while Lopez hummed at variance, favouring old Mexican melodies. Marvin gave up after a while, and sheer tiredness brought the prisoners to silence. Before they slept, they exchanged a few words.

'Say Drifter, did you really meet up

with those folks back there in the wagon?'

'Sure, I did. An' that girl, Cipriana, is the prettiest thing I ever did see on two legs. As far as I'm concerned, she's the treasure located with the wagoners. Now shut-up, will you? My thoughts are a whole lot more interestin' than your talk.'

For a time Lopez tried to read the expression on his cousin's face, but it wasn't easy with Drifter's hat tilted forward over his features. Left with his own thoughts, the Texican wondered how deep an impression the girl had made upon his partner. This far, he had never thought of Drifter as being at all interested in women. Maybe he had misread him, all along. Maybe he had the right sort of feelings to quit the trails at some time in the future. Could be he was the settling type, after all.

★　★　★

Breakfast was a peaceable affair, with the prisoners getting their fair share of

111

the bacon, biscuits and beans. It was only when the time for clearing up came around that Drifter perceived that their captors had made up their minds about him.

He was to be left behind.

'Why don't I go along with you?' he protested, as he hopped about with his ankles tied.

Graft and Marvin came away from the horses, which they had been saddling and stood before him. The older man looked at the younger who shrugged. Graft explained.

'We're takin' Lopez in for money, amigo. You must know that. You ain't worth anything to us, otherwise the banker an' the marshal would have known something about your tricky little ways. If you hadn't treated us badly, we would have cut you in on a third of the reward money. Seein' as how you left us in the lurch, you don't qualify no more.'

Clamping his hat on his bald head, Marvin said his little piece.

'Seein' as how we don't want you around when we collect the money, we're takin' your horse along with us. You'll be hoofin' it around here for a while. I hope it keeps fine for you.'

Bristling with anger, Drifter hauled on his bonds to no avail. Lopez grinned at him unsympathetically, while Graft scratched his greying thatch of fair hair. Drifter wondered if it was worthwhile pleading with the older man, but Graft merely ran his thumb between his paunch and his waistbelt and burped.

'But if you take my horse that amounts to theft! You know what sort of a hot reception horse thieves get in this part of the west!'

Graft merely shrugged. 'If anyone asks us, we'll tell them we were only borrowing your cayuse. That ought to satisfy most folks. After all, we're doin' the townsmen a favour.'

Drifter looked as if he was about to spring on Graft, even with his ankles tied. Marvin gave him a mean look. 'You want we should take your boots with us, as well?' he queried.

With that, Drifter backed off and sat down, turning his wrath on Lopez.

'Seems you're in something of a fix, amigo,' the latter remarked unfeelingly. 'Before you say anything, recollect that you have not always been well disposed towards me.'

'I hope you rot in that cell, or get your neck stretched,' Drifter retorted bitterly.

Drifter's cutting words reminded Lopez of the uncertainty of his own future. He tried to make amends.

'Shucks, don't take on so. I hope we both meet soon in far better circumstances, an' those are words right from my heart!'

Lopez knew that if Drifter did not intervene on his behalf his future could be short and perilous.

'If the worst comes to the worst, I could always put some flowers on your grave,' Drifter murmured.

Lopez sighed, knowing that the ties of blood were likely to work in his favour after Drifter had recovered from his present situation.

They left him by the fire as they had promised. Some distance up the track, but still in sight, they threw aside one of his revolvers and scattered a handful of bullets. Drifter watched them go out of sight and then he turned his attention to his first problem, that of getting the strings off his ankles and wrists.

★ ★ ★

Dusty, but with a show of arrogant pride, Graft and Marvin jogged up the main street of Rio City with their prisoner between them. Long before they reached the peace office up the west end, they had a crowd around them. A handful of young boys pranced around in the rear of the plodding horses, while older people hurried along the sidewalks on either side and tried to get confirmation from the two armed riders that their prisoner was

115

indeed the recent robber of the local bank.

Graft and Marvin maintained silence until the bulky figure of O'Halloran appeared on the sidewalk outside his office. The peace officer's eyes were never away from Lopez as he enquired who he was.

'The bank robber, Lopez,' Graft announced, as he dismounted.

'We were at the cabin where you met the man called Drifter, an' we heard the banker offer a thousand dollars for bringing in this criminal alive,' Marvin added.

The marshal nodded. He wiped his hands down the front of his buckskin tunic and roughly assisted the welcome prisoner out of the saddle. Lopez was hustled indoors, followed by his captors. The cell door in the rear of the office had closed upon the newcomer before those who had brought him had the time to look around.

O'Halloran indicated upright chairs and gave them a frosty look. Fuente came in and was sent for the banker, who arrived within five minutes and produced the promised reward from the inside pocket of his jacket. Graft counted it and thanked him.

'There was no loot on him when we found him, Mr. Denver, but my pardner an' me, we would like to help recover it for you.'

Denver was shaking his head before all Graft's words were uttered.

'That won't be necessary, my friend. All that remains for you to do is to leave town promptly and forget about the whole incident. In fact I'm makin' that a condition of the payment.'

Graft looked stunned by this pronouncement. Marvin opened his mouth to protest, but his partner intervened and ushered him out into the open air.

8

Back on trail and very frustrated, Drifter gave vent to his feelings. He cursed fluently in the American tongue, and when he grew tired of using the language of the trails he started off again with a series of cutting Spanish oaths. In his travels with Lopez and others he had picked up quite a lot of the Latin tongue used south of the border. In ordinary circumstances, however, he was a little reluctant to talk in Spanish owing to the fact that a lot of the phraseology he had picked up was not fit for the ears of respectable people.

Five minutes later, he began to calm down. He needed to be free without delay.

A few of the sticks on the fire still had life in them. He could use fire to free himself, or, he could hop along the track with his ankles still trussed, search for his revolver and load it up with the scattered ammunition and shoot off his bonds.

Possible embarrassment made him put aside the latter idea. He would look a fool if anyone spotted him hopping up the trail, even if help was offered. So, he applied himself to the fire. By the time he had contrived to burn through the thong holding his legs together his limbs ached and one of his boots had acquired a burn mark which no amount of brushing and polishing would get rid of.

He found himself wondering why he had not freed his wrists first, but decided not to trouble his head with such conjecture. Freeing his hands took a little less time, but the skin of his wrists was slightly raw in places where the thong had chafed.

No other travellers appeared as he plodded up the track and began the search for his gun. He was not a gunman by inclination, but he felt naked with his right hand holster flopping emptily against his thigh. Presently, his questing eyes noticed a bullet standing up on end. Others were recovered within a short time. The gun, itself, remained hidden for almost a quarter of an hour and when he sighted it, it was deeply embedded in a sizeable green bush amply defended by sharp unyielding thorns of more than an inch in length.

Consequently, his boots were badly scuffed and his hands, lacking gauntlets, acquired a few painful scratches before the firearm was recovered. He turned his thoughts back to the time when Marvin had hurled aside the gun. He decided that Red Marvin had a mean streak in him, and that if their trails ever happened to cross again the red-headed man would have to suffer.

To reload the revolver was the work of only a minute or two. After that, there was thinking to do. Drifter still had the makings with him. He pulled out his tobacco sack, his papers and a match stick and calmly built himself two cigarettes. One he lit immediately, and the other he placed inside his hat.

He thought about Lopez, Graft and Marvin going off up the trail to Rio City, the latter pair to collect the thousand dollars which *he* had schemed for. The blood pulsed through his veins again as vicious thoughts occupied his mind. He forced himself to be calm to think objectively.

He decided that Lopez had time in hand, provided he was not in any hurry to tell the banker what he wanted to know about his missing bank funds. Lopez could survive long enough for a friend to get into town and bring about his escape. It was not at all clear whether the Texican had told the truth about the loot, and that was highly unsatisfactory. Nevertheless, it had been their intention for Lopez to be taken into custody and then spirited away again.

Drifter knew that he could not let his partner down, even though he was completely out of sympathy with him. If they had to part company it would have to be in the future, not now. Another factor which would have taken the young Texan to Rio was the theft of his horse. He wanted it back again before anyone had a chance to sell it.

Rio City was due for a visit from him and for some action. He glanced back down the track leading to the south, wondering how long before the first transport heading north came along.

★ ★ ★

There was a plank six feet in length attached to the wall at the rear of Lopez's cell. In ordinary circumstances, the occupier of the cell was entitled to use it as a bed. Not often was it used in the daytime, but Lopez was an unusual character.

In his calmest mood, he stretched out on it. With his hands behind his head he contemplated the cracked ceiling for a while. After that, apparently oblivious to the comings and goings in the office, he closed his eyes and simulated sleep. For a time, Fuente stayed in the office.

Banker Denver called O'Halloran out into the street and had a private chat with him. Now that he had a definite lead to the missing loot, Mark S. Denver was able to call upon patience. All he wanted to be assured about was that they had the right man. The marshal convinced him, and that was sufficient to send the banker back to his business to attend to a few pressing chores.

When O'Halloran returned to the office around midday, he was carrying a tray of food with a cover over it. He stepped inside, gestured for Fuente to leave the building and put the tray down on his desk. Presently, Lopez's nose twitched. He had smelled the food.

He blinked his eyes, turned his head, smiled and nodded to the marshal. The latter unlocked the cell door, retreated to the desk and carried the tray into the cell with a six-gun in his hand.

Lopez came to his feet smoothly while the door was being locked again. He picked up the tray, carried it to his all-purpose bench and uncovered it. He glanced appreciatively at the beef and two vegetables and a plate of fruit pie.

'You provide a good meal, marshal,' he remarked conversationally.

While O'Halloran pretended to be busy at his desk, the Texican fixed his bandanna in the front of his shirt and unconcernedly started to eat. He had finished the first course when he spoke again.

'Are you thinkin' of chargin' me with something, marshal? I'd say the preliminaries are a little overdue.'

The marshal's bleached brows shot up his forehead. 'Shucks, Lopez, you're a cool customer. Especially as I have your picture on my desk.'

'My picture?' Lopez queried, his mouth full of fruit pie.

The peace officer chuckled without humour. He picked up the reward notice, crossed to the cell door and slipped it underneath. 'Are you goin' to argue that this fellow is not you?'

Lopez emptied his mouth and clicked his tongue. 'It's not a good likeness of anybody. Surely you don't think it's me? There's been a mistake somewhere along the line. Those hombres who brought me in were jest after the reward. They talked of nothin' else after they jumped me on the trail south. Nope, this ain't me. You can be sure of it.'

The prisoner resumed his eating.

'So you're not a wanted robber, an' you never attacked the Rio an' Laredo Bank in this town?'

'That's about the size of things, marshal. I'm jest a citizen of the United States passin' through.'

Marshal O'Halloran stiffened in his chair, making it creak. He thrust a warning finger in the prisoner's direction. 'Now see here, Lopez, we can put the pressure on you jest as soon as we feel like it, so don't push your luck! You won't be actin' smart when we face you up with that bank teller. You got close enough to him to hit him over the head with a pistol. After that, you fixed him with a gag so he nearly choked to death! But he's still around, an' he'll know you. Believe me, he'll only need one glance.'

The prisoner finished his food. He burped politely, carried the empty tray towards the door and retired again. He knew and O'Halloran knew the type of man the teller was. He wore thick-lensed spectacles.

Glancing idly through the street window, the Texican observed: 'In my experience long-service bank tellers usually have poor eyesight. I wouldn't build up on anything, if I were you. When the real robber is apprehended you'd be in a fix, if you'd mistreated me. Maybe that's why you're pushin' good food my way, an' treadin' carefully.'

Suddenly angered, O'Halloran sprang to his feet. He hurled his big side-rolled grey stetson at a rack in a corner. It missed the hooks and rolled on the floor. Lopez watched this phenomenon with acute politeness.

'Now see here, you ornery coyote, if we want to we can fix it for two or three bank employees to identify you beyond a shadow of doubt! An' I mean positive identifications, so don't act so smart from here on in!'

Lopez sat down on his bench, made a steeple of his fingers and glanced regretfully in the peace officer's direction. He shook his head and clicked his tonque.

'Such an unexpected outburst. So contrary to the sort of justice expected by an honest citizen. Marshal, I truly hope your words were not heard by anyone outside of the building. In some towns, you could be thrown out of office for usin' threats like that. I'm sure that wasn't the true you talkin'. I can't think what must have come over you.'

O'Halloran punched the back of his chair, sending it spinning. Lopez offered him his reward notice back, but he ignored the gesture. Snatching up his hat, he stormed out of the office and stood on the sidewalk consumed by anger.

Fuente came back presently. O'Halloran warned him to take no chances with the prisoner. 'I'm goin' to speak with Denver. I won't be long.'

The townsfolk, who had often seen their marshal in an angry mood, studied his face as he stalked along and gave him plenty of room. He went straight to the back door of the Rio and Laredo, knocked and was asked to step inside.

Denver was always a striking figure with his shaven head and neat tailored clothes. On this occasion, his small mouth was a tight slit under his beak of a nose. His hollowed green eyes showed his alertness, and few would have realised that he was troubled.

'Well, marshal? You've had a chance to look him over now. What's his general attitude?'

O'Halloran scowled. He removed his hat and hung it up before manoeuvring his long body towards the visitor's seat on the near side of the black-topped desk.

'Would a glass of wine help?' Denver prompted. He pushed a carafe of red wine and a glass in his visitor's direction.

The marshal as a rule did not drink wine. He sniffed and prepared to refuse the offer, but at the last minute he decided to accept. When he had sipped, he looked the banker in the eye and tried to set his thoughts in order.

'If you ask me, Mr. Denver, he's altogether too calm. Claims the picture on the reward notice is not him. Says a mistake has been made. Hints that your teller would have difficulty in identifying him. That sort of thing. I think we might have to put quite a bit of pressure on him to find out what you want to know.'

'You've fed him well?'

'Sure he didn't leave a scrap. Said

complimentary things about the food. Made me lose my temper, as well.'

'Maybe we could starve him into a better frame of mind. Then I ought to have a go at getting him to talk, myself. He'll have a weakness of some sort. We'll get through to him, never fear.'

Denver was smiling thinly when the marshal started to shake his head. The banker, who did not like to be crossed, subtly changed his expression. He waited for an explanation.

'You were sayin' about havin' a weakness,' the marshal explained. 'This far I haven't given him anything to drink. He'll be askin', an' I have a notion he's likely to be a drinkin' man. Rather than starve him, maybe we ought to give him a fair amount to drink.'

Denver relaxed again. 'What then? Beer, whiskey? What should we try on him?'

'This wine of yours is fairly potent. I was thinkin' we might try him on wine.

What do you say? Could we run to that?'

Showing his most amiable side, Denver remarked: 'With what we have at stake, you could use a gallon on him, if necessary. So long as he doesn't pass out altogether. Leave him for a while, until he's good an' thirsty. Then take him a bottle in. Fix it with the nearest bar. Charge it to my account.'

Having finished his drink, the marshal rose to his feet. He hesitated, shrugged and collected his hat.

'Was there something else?' Denver prompted.

'I was jest goin' to remark that I've seen no sign of that fellow who particularly wanted to get his hands on Lopez. Fellow named Drifter. He could probably have made him talk. But maybe the wine will do the trick. I'll put him in one of the corridor cells. You could interrogate him down there. We've no other prisoners in at the moment.'

Denver saw him to the door. 'Very

well. I'll make myself available when you think the time is ripe. Just send me a message.'

O'Halloran stepped outside looking far more confident than when he had arrived.

9

Drifter's impatience considerably added to his tribulations on the way into Rio City. In the hour after he started up the trail on foot no one overtook him from the south. His riding boots which were very comfortable for riding in started to pinch his feet as he walked on the rough surface trail.

Around half past nine, a short stocky character with skin the colour of mahogany and a wispy white beard heralded his approach from the south by whistling a catchy Confederacy marching tune. Drifter stopped when he heard it and sat down on a rock to await the newcomer.

Drury was the name of the old prospector. He had with him a mule which looked to have plenty of bottom, but he preferred to walk and allow his surefooted beast simply to carry his bedroll and a knapsack.

'You lookin' for company, young fellow?' he enquired as soon as he overtook Drifter.

The young man managed a smile. 'Sure, I can do with some company, old timer. The fact is, a couple of hombres went off with my horse early this mornin' an' I have to get to Rio as soon as possible.'

'Well, I'll be glad to walk along with you, if my company will help. Sometimes, if you have someone to talk to it helps to lessen the burden on the feet.'

Drifter began to step it out, and soon he was hearing various tales of lurid exploits in a Confederacy infantry battalion during the Civil War. For a time, he listened with interest. Soon, however, the aching of his feet made the old man's voice seem monotonous.

'Something botherin' you, son?' Drury asked, at the end of a lengthy story.

'Only my feet, pardner. How would it be if I took a lift on the back of your burro for a while?'

Drury stroked his beard. 'Well, he ain't all that keen on carryin' strangers, I guess.'

'I'd make it worth your while. How about a couple of dollars for the ride?'

Drury blinked hard, made his mind up and held out his hand. Drifter fished two one dollar bills out of the back of his shirt and gratefully handed them over. The old man held them up to the sunlight, as though to make sure they were genuine. Having satisfied himself, he stopped the burro, removed the knapsack and bedroll and gestured for Drifter to mount him.

The burro bucked about a bit, but permitted Drifter to straddle him. For perhaps a furlong all went well. Then, as Drury started to whistle a particularly catchy tune, the beast suddenly went berserk, throwing up his hind legs this way and that, and finally making off into the scrub with a total disregard for the comfort and safety of its rider.

Drifter called out for help, but all

that the prospector did was laugh loudly in a high-pitched voice. The mule careered on for two hundred yards before finally jerking him over its head into a patch of stones and prickly bushes. The young Texan's senses slipped away as his head connected with a boulder.

When he recovered, the mule had gone, along with its owner. A buckboard came up from the south half an hour later. It was travelling at a good speed. Drifter was still wide of the trail when he heard its approach. He called out hoarsely to no avail. Eventually, he fired off a couple of shots into the air to attract attention, but the driver of the vehicle merely increased speed as he was startled by the gunfire.

Some time in the early afternoon, an elderly Mexican couple came along in a cart. They were quite willing to help him, but they insisted on having a siesta by the trailside before going on.

Drifter parted company with them, as they appeared to have no inclination to get a move on at all, but later on they overtook him again and he was glad to take a lift in the back of the cart. He was so exhausted and out of sorts with himself that he fell asleep and did not recover until after dark in the Mexican part of the town to which he was heading.

He was invited to partake of a simple meal, which he accepted. After that, he smoked a couple of cigarettes and turned in again, using a borrowed blanket. He breakfasted off *tortilla* pancakes and coffee around eight o'clock the following morning, and only then began to investigate the fate of Lopez and the whereabouts of his horse.

He avoided a direct approach to the peace office, and made use of the cafes and bars for his information. Within half an hour, he was assured that Lopez was behind bars and being well fed for the moment. Satisfied that no one was in any hurry to rush his reckless cousin to the hanging tree, he then began further enquiries about horses.

In each of the three main liveries he asked questions about his own horse, giving its description in detail and suggesting that it was lost and that someone might have brought it in and left it. The sorrel was nowhere around. Neither was Lopez's roan, or the mounts of Graft and Marvin.

An old man smoking a pipe on a sidewalk bench informed him that the two strangers who had brought in the bank robber had left town almost at once. That was disappointing news. If they had moved on, almost certainly his sorrel had been taken along with them.

He was almost ready to give up when an idea occurred to him. All his searching and questioning since breakfast-time had been in the Texan half of the town. He decided now to make a few more enquiries among the regular Mexican families who occupied the adobes.

And there his luck changed. He gravitated towards the biggest *cantina*, drawn by the sounds of music and the click of castanets. In an alcove to one side of the bar, a lithe young Spanish girl of sixteen or seventeen years was doing a sinewy traditional dance to the accompaniment of a pair of guitarists who might very well have been father and son.

Perhaps a score of Mexicans were sitting at the nearby tables, drinking, clapping and applauding. The snap of the girl's heels and the rhythmic clicking of the castanets went quicker and quicker. Although the girl was attractive, Drifter had only eyes for the white American feasting his bloodshot eyes on her from one of the nearest tables.

Red Marvin, who had a taste for Mexican women and the Latin style of entertainment, had defied the banker's instructions regarding leaving town. For the first time that day, Drifter began to feel confident. Now that he had located Marvin, he felt that his luck would change. The dance finished. All the Mexicans waved their drinking mugs, or stood up and waved their hats. For a time, it looked as if Marvin would be eclipsed by the general clamour of the Mexican males, but when the girl started to move between the tables, he reached out and grabbed her by the wrist, insisting that she should sit at his table and drink.

The girl glanced around at the proprietor, who first shrugged and then signalled his approval of the move. Another carafe of wine appeared on Marvin's table, along with a fresh glass. He poured for both of them, and at once toasted the dancer heartily.

Drifter knew a malicious satisfaction when the redhead's speech became excessively slurred. Quite soon afterwards, Red's trunk tilted forward over the table. His hat came off, revealing his bald head. The young dancer seemed disconcerted. She picked up his hat as he started to snore and looked around for assistance. None came from the Mexicans, but Drifter was quick to seize his chance.

He sauntered over and touched his hat. 'Buenos dias, señorita. Red Marvin is a friend of mine. As he seems to have passed out, I'll be glad to assist him along to his lodgings till he feels better. Would that be all right?'

She hesitated. 'Oh, er, si, señor. Thank you very much.'

Drifter explained that he had only just arrived in town, and he was told the location of the adobe where Marvin had dossed down the night before. Marvin's legs did not work at all, and he had to be supported for almost two hundred yards. Drifter became excessively winded but his satisfaction in finding Marvin prevented him from giving up. At last he reached the door of the adobe. He paused there, and supported himself and his burden against the wall. A young Mexican woman emerged, carrying a basket of clean washing which she was taking to another part of the town.

'Buenos dias, señora,' Drifter greeted her. 'My friend has had too much of the vino. Will it be all right if I put him to bed an' stay with him for a while?'

His manner dispelled the young woman's doubts. She replied: 'Si, señor, por favor. I'll be back in an hour.'

She showed him the door to Marvin's room and left him alone. Drifter hoisted his burden indoors and tossed him on the low bed. He waited until he had recovered some of his breath, and then he applied himself to the task of rousing his victim.

First, he sat him up and shook him well. Marvin's teeth rattled, but he failed to recover. Next, the black vest was removed. Drifter was not at all surprised to discover in a pocket located in the lining a bundle of dollar bills amounting to over four hundred dollars. This, he removed, putting the cash inside his shirt.

In another room, he located a clay water jar with a narrow spout. This was used to flush the drunk's head, face and neck. After much spluttering, Marvin began to mutter and shake himself. The pressure of the revolver muzzle on his left ear did the rest.

The bleak expression on Drifter's face so close to his own did the rest.

'Howdy, friend Marvin. Long time no see. I wouldn't have troubled you a whole lot now, but I'm tired of walkin'. Where's my horse? A spot of fast talkin' will improve relations between us! Start talkin'.'

Marvin waved his hands about, obviously perplexed by his rude awakening. He glanced around, and saw that his guns and belt had been moved several feet away. A gentle pressure on the gun by his ear produced results.

'Shucks, you don't have to carry on like this! After all, we didn't intend you any real harm, Drifter.' Drifter moved a finger. 'It ain't — it ain't in town! It's with Graft. He's at a cabin north from Two Mile Rock. That's west of here.'

He went on to explain the route in great detail, and Drifter felt sure that he was telling the truth. Marvin's saddlery was in the room. A glance through a window showed that the skewbald was pegged out in a small corral round the back. Five minutes was long enough to truss the bald-headed man. When he was satisfied, he stepped back and studied the sorry figure.

'Amigo, the next time our trails cross, there'll be shootin'. Take my advice an' sleep for a while. Your landlady will be back shortly.'

So saying, Drifter tied a bandanna across the unfortunate man's mouth. He moved out, taking the saddle with him. The skewbald showed a certain amount of displeasure upon being mounted by a stranger, but it soon began to show proper respect.

★   ★   ★

The time was a little after noon when Drifter dismounted in the last of the trees before the clearing north of Two Mile Rock. He moved across the open ground with his revolver to hand. The first human sounds he heard amounted

144

to a series of bubbling snores. The door was open. The only occupant was Limpy Graft, who was stretched out on a long deal table, his head pillowed on his hat and two empty liquor bottles near at hand.

Drifter made no attempt to quieten his steps, but no sounds communicated themselves to the inebriated Graft, who snored on. Limpy's share of the spoils was tucked away in a pocket of one of the two saddles stacked against a wall. Upwards of four hundred and fifty dollars remained. Drifter transferred the money, along with a tobacco sack, papers, matches and a box of bullets to his own person.

He relaxed in a rocker long enough to smoke a cigarette and then he rose and prepared to leave. A vengeful feeling made him put the blanket and saddle on Graft's horse before he withdrew. The sorrel came out of the trees at the rear of the cabin to his whistle and gave him an affectionate snicker.

When he left he turned up the valley, taking the two spare horses with him. He forded a stream, drove them up the other side and caused enough commotion to send them running for a quarter of a mile or more. Only then did his thoughts go back to town and to Lopez's plight.

10

Rio City, being near the border with Mexico, indulged to a large extent in the habit of siesta. The town was relatively quiet by the time Drifter's sorrel carried him back into the centre towards two o'clock that same afternoon. He took a beer in a saloon, made himself look unobtrusive and listened to the gossip.

Lopez was still one of the main topics of conversation. One or two of the locals seemed to be baffled because no information had come out of the peace office appertaining to the loot which the robber was supposed to have removed from the bank.

At the other end of the long bar, a poker-faced barman with a cauliflower ear listened to the trading of conversation for a few minutes before inserting himself into the discussion.

'If you ask me, gents,' he began, in a stage whisper, 'I'd say Mr. Denver is bidin' his time about demandin' the information. It ain't generally known, but the marshal has taken in several bottles of wine to his office. Now, I happen to know he don't usually like wine, an' Fuente has complained more than once that he's not allowed to drink it, either.'

A rancher hooked his boot in the bar rail and answered. 'Are you suggestin' the wine is goin' in there for the prisoner?'

'It's not for me to say, mister, but I'd say O'Halloran is systematically loosenin' the road agent's tongue. Mind you, I wouldn't like to be quoted as havin' said such a thing, you understand.'

The conversation went on, but Drifter had heard enough. He wandered out of doors, mounted up again and did a circuit of the main streets. On his tour, he saw the rear of the peace office across the vacant lots from the street further north. Lopez's roan was pegged out on a patch of ground between the long cell block extension and a high wooden fence which separated the office land from that behind the building next door. A stack of horse jewelry was heaped against the cell block wall. It was probably that taken from the back of the roan. That gave him food for thought.

Back on Main, he exchanged words with a casual visitor to the office. 'How's the bank robber gettin' on in there?'

The visitor, a clerk from the mail office, shrugged his shoulders and answered off-handedly. 'How would I know, mister? He ain't in the cell that fronts on the office no more.'

More useful information. A trip up the east end of Main resulted in Drifter almost running into Mark Denver as the latter came out of the bank and started westward along the street. There was a look of grim purpose which showed about the mouth and eyes of the banker. His gait also suggested that he was on an errand of some importance.

Drifter cautiously stood the sorrel behind a standing cart with a high canvas top. The banker soon went by. The rider then turned back, keeping a distance of fifty yards between himself and his quarry. As soon as he was certain that the bank president was headed for the peace office, Drifter turned into an intersection and moved back on Second Street.

This time, he took the sorrel down a passage between buildings parallel with the peace office and dismounted. The cropping roan showed only mild interest as he cat-footed across the open space and stopped outside the wall of the cell block, listening for sounds coming through the open grilled windows a few feet above his head. There were three openings, in all. The only sounds came from the middle one. A familiar voice was raised in a quiet song. The words were slurred, as though through drink.

Distantly, the sounds of voices carried from the single grille in the back wall of the office proper. Denver was in there talking to someone. Unfortunately, the voices were muted sufficiently to be unintelligible.

Any sort of break-out was clearly out of the question while the banker and others were around the office. If an attempt to interrogate Lopez was about to take place, however, Drifter wanted if at all possible to be within earshot. Consequently, when he heard sounds which indicated a move from the office to the cell block, he stayed close, underneath the grille where he had heard Lopez's voice.

The door to the corridor opened with a clang. After that, it was possible to pick out most of what was being said. Drifter was surprised that Fuente, and not the marshal, was conducting the banker to the prisoner's cell. There was something significant about that course of action: something he could not fathom right away.

The peculiar metallic ringing of keys on a key-ring, and one key inserted in a metal lock made it quite clear that the banker had arrived, and that he was entering the cell to have his conversation there. Drifter's mouth quirked into a grin. He wondered if his eavesdropping would be interrupted, or observed.

* * *

As he entered the cell, Mark Denver was making a positive effort to look amiable. He had with him a large bottle of red wine and two slim-stemmed glasses which he held delicately, with a finger in each. He hovered just inside the door like a gentleman on his best manners, and his first move after that was to remove the large cream stetson which revealed his hairless shaved crown in all its shiny glory.

Lopez, who was slumped on the all-purpose bench attached to the wall, looked impressed in spite of himself.

While they looked at one another, Fuente negotiated the two doors from the office, bringing with him an upright chair for the banker's benefit.

Lopez was not slow to notice the fresh bottle of wine. His own which had been handed to him directly after a light breakfast, was practically empty. Denver held out the new bottle and the glasses, which he received eagerly and put down on the bench beside him.

In the meantime, Fuente was excusing himself to the banker for closing and locking the door behind him, and Denver was giving his surroundings a brief but thorough scrutiny. In the direction of the office, he could see all the way through the first cell to the rear of the office itself, but between the middle cell and the third was a screen from ceiling to floor, from the outer wall of the block to the inner wall which held the access door. The screen was crudely made of old Indian blankets long past their best. None of them was

153

sufficiently threadbare to be seen through.

'Good day to you, Lopez. I'd be obliged if you'd pour out for the two of us before we talk. In the heat of the day, ordinary conversation dries the throat. We don't have to suffer thirst, even if the interview is painful.'

Lopez nodded and grinned. He never needed to be asked twice to drink a glass of wine.

'That's uncommon decent of you, Mr. Denver,' he responded. 'I'd like to drink your health, an' I'd also like to think you have my best interests at heart.'

Denver received a glass and gave a chuckle. He raised it, clinked it against Lopez's glass and sipped it. 'As a matter of fact, your best interests can be served by frankness in this discussion. I have the authority in this town, its being close to the border with Mexico, to bring about a hasty execution for robbery with violence, if I feel that way inclined.

'This far, since you arrived, I've been lenient with you. No one has given you any sort of difficulty. Now, you have to come up with information. Your future depends upon how you respond. I have all the evidence I need as to your entering the premises of my bank, as to what you removed, and what happened to my chief teller.

'You're lucky not to be facin' a murder charge, but that's beside the point. You may not realise it as a robber of banks, but such establishments are not only there to house the savings of the local people. They are there as a safe resting place for the valuables of wealthy citizens. Anybody can use my bank as a depository. Do you understand?'

Lopez tilted back his head and drained his glass. He was grinning broadly and licking the drops of wine off his darkly-stubbled upper lip when his bloodshot eyes regarded those of his interrogator.

'Sure, sure, Mr. Denver. I understand

perfectly. A man doesn't have to be honest to deposit his goods in your bank.'

Denver was clearly annoyed by this rejoinder, but he covered it by leaning forward out of his chair and recharging Lopez's glass. The latter watched him fondly. His grin even broadened. Laughter shook him so that his gusty breath came near to intoxicating his visitor.

'Truly, Lopez, you have the mind of a criminal. Perhaps I'm bein' too patient with you.'

'Could be, could be,' the prisoner assured him, as he raised his glass with extreme care and examined it against the light. 'I explained to the marshal yesterday that I don't think you have a jot of evidence against me, an' all he suggested was that witnesses could and would be found, an' that amounts to corruption if I have the right word.'

Denver's voice was sharper when he resumed. 'If you don't want to be put away forever, listen, you fool. The man who deposited that box which you stole has since died. He had a fatal accident in a town north of here.'

'Would that be the jasper they called El Mestizo?' Lopez queried, genuinely interested.

'The man I'm speaking of was a decent salesman, an' no sort of brigand, if that's what you're tryin' to say. It is because of his death that I am so keen to get back what you took away!'

'You know what they say about El Mestizo, Mr. Denver?'

'I don't gossip about bandits, an' I don't want to know what others say about the one you keep mentioning. Now, where was I? Oh, yes, that silver cross, the chalice stowed away with it of the same metal, and the oil painting were all the possessions of a wealthy private citizen.

'You have brought dishonour on the bank by spiriting them away. *I* have to get them back to restore the prestige of my establishment. Do you understand my position? I *have* to have them back!

157

Those items and the money that was with them!'

Lopez shook with silent laughter. He could not remember when he had enjoyed an interview so much. It took some little time for him to get control of himself, but he succeeded after a while.

'El Mestizo was said to be mad on gold, mister. He wouldn't have bothered with a silver crucifix or a silver chalice. All he wanted was the yellow metal. Now, he *would* have been interested in a gold crucifix, encrusted with precious stones, or a golden bowl, or even a beautiful old picture of the Madonna and Child. Those sort of items, along with say, fifty thousand dollars could make the basis of a man's fortune. I could understand you bein' upset if you'd lost items such as I've jest described, but silver trinkets? Not likely, amigo.'

All through this last speech. Lopez's eyelids had been growing heavier and heavier. Suddenly at the end of his talk an overbearing tiredness took possession. He started to keel over on the bench, and Denver had to reach for the bottle before it was knocked over.

'Fancy . . . fancy losin' El Mestizo's golden loot. An' an' threatin' to keep me locked up forever. Me, I couldn't do a thing to help. Not from the inside of a cell. What a pity. A pity for the bandit, a pity for the banker. A pity for me . . . '

He was rather far gone towards sleep when a sudden noise on the other side of the curtain startled him. The sound of a boot hitting the floor. The rather harsh noise which Marshal O'Halloran made when he cleared his throat came from the same place. Lopez fought his weariness long enough to see the tall peace officer walk out of the adjoining cell and address himself to the banker.

'What do you think, Mr. Denver?'

Denver shrugged. 'Oh, I found out all I wanted to know, for the present. He's described just about every item in the box. So he must know its value and where it is.'

'My sentiments exactly, sir,' O'Halloran agreed. 'I think I know what our next move is likely to be.'

He yelled for Fuente to return with the key, while Lopez tried to figure when — unknown to him — the marshal had slipped behind the blanket screen unnoticed. The prisoner decided that it must have been around one p.m. when he was briefly allowed out to answer a call of nature.

Although his mind was sluggish, he had a feeling that he had not done himself a lot of good in what he had said to his visitor. The drunken stupor prevented him from worrying about the problem.

11

Rio City possessed but one law office. The name of the qualified attorney was Wilberforce Brace. He had a building on Second Street which combined business offices and living quarters. It ran to two storeys in height and was flanked on all sides by small beds of flowers and neat small bush fences.

Wil Brace, thought by some to have been around as long as Rio was a city, was in his sixty-seventh year. For ten years he had been a widower. Since his wife died, he had been self-sufficient. His small but lucrative law practice had made enough money for him to retire and live reasonably well. Consequently, he never went looking for business, and spent a lot of his time reading through the select library of literature left to him by his father. In appearance he was a colourful figure. His grey hair was thin and parted high. His face had a lean and leathery look partially camouflaged by broad side whiskers. His rather pale grey eyes were almost always behind the lenses of his gold-rimmed spectacles which had the effect of magnifying his irises. When he left his office to move around the town he was seen habitually in a tall beaver hat and a grey frockcoat. His tailored trousers were of a lighter grey.

He was seated in a wing-backed armchair poring over a volume of European history when Mark Denver ascended the outside staircase at five o'clock that afternoon and rang the bell.

Brace rose to his feet without haste, but his welcome was cordial enough when he opened the door and ushered the banker inside. A carafe of wine stood on the table. The lawyer poured for them both and handed over one glass. 'First time I've seen you this month, Mark. Here's to your health, in the best madeira!'

Denver smiled. 'And to yours, old friend. You always did keep the best wine cellar in town.'

They drank and seated themselves, and when the pleasantries were over, Lawyer Brace asked an obvious question. 'How are you getting on with your prisoner? The one who robbed your bank, I mean.'

'Well, he isn't my prisoner, really, Wil, as you can well appreciate. He's O'Halloran's for the moment. By the way, I've asked the marshal to step around this evening and listen in on our talk. I hope you don't mind?'

Brace shrugged and made a placatory gesture with his hand. 'Only too pleased, to be sure. In fact, I'm glad of the company. Always reading and never conversing with one's fellows tends to dull the wits. Besides, O'Halloran is a good lawman for this town. He deserves a bit of encouragement. But I think you were going to tell me about your robber.'

After drawing his chair a little closer,

Denver explained all that had transpired between himself and Lopez earlier that same afternoon. Brace asked a few questions about Lopez's earlier career, and the banker filled him in on the little he knew.

'So you're convinced beyond doubt that he really did steal that treasure box and that he knows what was in it?'

Denver chuckled grimly. 'In his liquored state, he described the crucifix in some detail. Also the chalice, and the oil painting of the Madonna and Child, And he knew the exact amount of money stashed away in big bills. Moreover, he mentioned the name of El Mestizo as if he was familiar with him, or at least with his ways.'

At this juncture, O'Halloran bounced up the wooden staircase, hat in hand, knocked and admitted himself. Brace produced beer for him and indicated a padded chair for him to take. When the peace officer was settled in, the lawyer resumed the conversation.

'I was about to ask Mr. Denver, here,

if he had heard any more about El Mestizo of late.'

The marshal declined the offer of a cigar, and, instead, rolled himself a cigarette. 'We haven't heard any more since that report of last month which came through from the Arizona Rangers. As you know, Mr. Brace, a party of rangers claimed that El Mestizo was trapped between their posse and a sharpshootin' bunch of *rurales* who had chased the bandits across the Rio Grande.

'One or two bodies were recovered, but not that of El Mestizo, himself. They believe, an' I think they're right when they say it, he was one of the two men unhorsed whose bodies went down a cataract an' were not recovered.'

Brace removed ash from his cigar into a cut glass ash tray. 'In that case, he may never be back to claim the missing treasure, which is almost certainly his. I wonder if that accident to the fellow who brought it into the bank was really an accident? I suppose it is quite possible the border bandit was getting rid of a fellow who knew too much about his business?'

Denver made a gesture with his cigar. 'It's the way criminals work, Wil. You know the criminal mind better than we do.'

There was a short pause after that observation. The main business of the evening was about to be discussed.

'I'm sure,' the lawyer began, 'that uppermost in your mind is the recovery of that treasure box. How will you make that fellow, Lopez, take you to the spot where he's buried it? He can hardly be taken along at gun point. What will you do?'

Denver eyed both his listeners keenly. Before he spoke his jaw muscles rippled as he pressed his teeth together.

'As you say, Wil, he can hardly be taken along at gun point. I think between us, O'Halloran an' I are goin' to have to bend the law a little. We have to engineer his escape. We'll need about three absolutely reliable men to go along with him under the guise of bank guards. Preferably men from out of town.'

'I know a trio of operators in Laredo. I could telegraph them this evenin' an' have them come along to Rio as soon as possible.'

O'Halloran rubbed out the butt of his cigarette rather thoroughly and observed the nicotine stain on his middle finger. 'I don't know when you plan to have him out, Mr. Denver. Could I remind you that he's full of good wine at this time. He'll need to sober up before there's any thought of an escape plan.'

'Yes, yes, of course, marshal. We'll give him time to sober up. Stop giving him any sort of liquor from this time forward. I reckon it will have to be the day after tomorrow, to give the men from Laredo time to get here. Do you think this is a good plan, Wil?'

The lawyer studied his cigar very closely without raising his eyes. 'In the circumstances, yours is as good a plan as any *I* could think of. Of course, there'll be other details you'll want to discuss with the marshal, here. I mean about after the box has been recovered. Or maybe that's only for the ears of the guards.'

Denver nodded and smiled rather grimly, while O'Halloran leaned forward and twiddled his thumbs.

★ ★ ★

Meanwhile, Drifter was sitting at a remote table in the Border saloon with a shot glass in his hand and a half full bottle of whiskey. He had heard all he wanted to know about the exchanges between Lopez and Denver. The sounds of O'Halloran's boots had not escaped him. He had deduced correctly that Lopez's revelations had been made in front of a witness who had heard it all.

Uppermost in the banker's mind could only be one thing: the recovery of the treasure box which only Lopez could lead them to. The Texican had been drunk when he talked, but Drifter felt sure that he would not easily reveal what he had done with the box. He would know that his days were numbered as soon as he had given the banker and his associates the information they wanted.

Therefore, he would have to be sprung. They would have to contrive his escape. Even if he talked while still in the cell, they could not be sure that he was telling the truth until the treasure was recovered. So, they were bound to have him go after it himself. If and when he was allowed to escape, Denver's men would be either with him, or in reasonably close touch with him, when he made his move to recover the loot.

Clearly, Lopez's mind was too fuddled for them to offer him the chance of escape the same day. It would have to be the next day or, possibly, the day after that. Drifter believed that he had summed up the situation accurately.

Now, he had to make up his mind as to his own course of action. Obviously the wagoners were the key to the loot's present whereabouts. If they didn't have it, it was somewhere near one of their resting places. Had he been pushed to find it alone, Drifter thought he might have stood an even chance of recovering it.

All the time he was thinking, he knew that he had to make some sort of a positive move to assist his partner in crime. Even if Lopez had thought seriously about abandoning *him* after finding the gold hoard, this was not the time to abandon a cousin to the consequences of his wrong-doings.

Lopez would have to be sprung, according to the terms of a long-standing promise. He thought of the ramifications of the treasure. It was, as Lopez had suggested, of great value. Would its lure be the means of driving a wedge between the two of them? Would it sour their relationship which had lasted for a long time?

And what of the wagoners involved? If they found out that Lopez was a common robber, would their attitude towards him change? Mention of a crucifix, a chalice and an oil painting of the Madonna and Child suggested loot taken from a church. Would they assume that he was a common church robber? They could be forgiven for making such an elementary mistake.

If they had the loot, then a lot depended upon whether they looked inside the mystery box. The man Joseph, he felt sure, would have very definite views on vandalism. So would the others. He had not known them long enough to be sure how they would react. In fact, on reflection he did not know how he was going to react himself to sudden wealth.

Due to the uncertainties of his family life, which had been terminated early, he had never been a regular churchgoer. But his parents, he felt sure, had a special sort of attitude towards churches, churchgoers and priests.

His cigarette stub burned down as far as his fingers. He bent down and rubbed it out on the sole of his boot. He thought again, in a more personal way, of the great value of a gold crucifix studded with precious stones. Was that the sort of object which a robber could sell for gain without a qualm of conscience?

Who would buy it? Would it have to be melted down and sold for its value as precious metal? He smiled to himself over his abysmal ignorance of anything of great value. He studied the colour of two fingers of amber liquid. His eyes held a vacant look as he visualised once again the shapely Cipriana's copper-tinted hair and violet eyes.

This business of the loot held one bonus in store for him. If all went well he would at least see the attractive girl once again. Always assuming that the Carreras' wagon could be located again. The possibility that it might not be easy to find gave him a few moments of acute anxiety. He was aware of new feelings of great depth: feelings that had never bothered him before.

If he made a mess of the rescue bid, he could finish up a prisoner alongside of his cousin. He sipped the spirit and presently his mood of pessimism passed. A visit to the peace office would have been useful, except that his face was known. Above all, he did not want to promote any curiosity in those who had already met him.

Ideas were slow to form as to how the rescue was to be mounted. Instead of drinking much time away, he left the building and made a tour of the town on foot.

12

Although Drifter wrestled with the problem of the rescue attempt for over an hour before he fell asleep that night, the exact details as to how the escape was to be perpetrated eluded him. All he knew for sure was that he would attempt it.

He slept late and ate a hearty breakfast before giving his mind to it again. It was around ten o'clock in the morning when he was seated on a bench across the street from the peace office reading a newspaper that the first glimmerings as to how it was to be done occurred to him.

Denver did not go near the office that morning. The whole town seemed to be waiting for some sort of development in the career of the bank robber. It was generally known that the circuit judge who tried important cases was not expected for several weeks. As Denver had made no move to invoke the local law and have the fellow strung up, the average townsman had no clear idea of what was about to happen.

The banker was noted for his aloofness. No one thought to ask him openly about a matter which was clearly the bank's private business. One or two casual visitors dropped in upon the marshal, but none of them stayed for long. Fuente, the Mexican deputy, went in and out. So did the marshal. They were obviously keeping a sharp lookout over the prisoner and awaiting some sort of advice from elsewhere.

Drifter decided to make his move around noon, or shortly afterwards when one or the other of the two peace officers was away from the building taking his lunch. At half past eleven, he started to put his plan into action.

His first move was to collect his sorrel from the livery. This he did without creating any fuss. He walked the sorrel around the north end of town, gradually working his way nearer to the next thoroughfare north of Main. When a suitable opportunity occurred, he slipped the horse down an alley which gave onto the land behind the peace office, and tethered it to a hook in a fence.

Next, he catfooted for the second time up the bit of meadow behind the offices. He caught Lopez's roan without making very much noise. Saddling it was a bit on the tricky side, but he managed that as well.

A few short sharp whistles alerted Lopez, who moved over to the grille and gave cautious notice of his presence.

'That you cousin?' the husky voice called out.

'Who else would be fool enough to saddle up your horse within shoutin' distance of the peace office?' Drifter called back. 'Get yourself ready for a quick move. Your cayuse is saddled an' some fool has left your weapons out here, as well. You okay?'

'But of course I'm okay, cousin. Especially since I've heard your voice. How are you goin' to do it?'

'I'm goin' in through the front. Don't give me any advice, an' don't hesitate when the time comes. I'm goin' away now. If anything goes wrong with this bid, you'll have to wait for the banker's men to spring you.'

'You know I always prefer your company to any other,' Lopez remarked, waxing loquacious.

But Drifter had already moved away, so that his voice did not carry. The Texan was excited now that the break was close. He found himself slightly breathless without benefit of exertion. Five minutes later, he emerged into Main Street and surveyed the front of O'Halloran's office from fifty yards away. It was as well he did not stare, because the marshal himself came out at that moment and stood for a minute or so talking earnestly to Carlos Fuente.

O'Halloran shrugged his shoulders a

time or two, made a big gesture with one hand and set off up the street towards the west end. Fuente watched him for a few seconds more before strolling back indoors rubbing his ample midriff as though he was hungry.

So Fuente had to be drawn out of the building. Drifter strolled up the street until the marshal opened the door of a cafe. Two hundred yards separated the eating house from the peace office. The young Texan crossed the street with his hand held up to his face, in case O'Halloran was in a position to pick out faces through the steamed-up window glass. He made as if to enter, and then walked on past. Ten yards further on, an impatient farmer sitting the box of his cart, took delivery of a box of provisions carried by a scrawny teenage youth who had barely been able to stagger along with it.

The lad touched his straw hat hopefully but all he got for his pains was a venomous look. The farmer flicked his whip over the team and pulled away from the sidewalk. Drifter sidled along to the door of the cafe while the lad hovered on the boards, uncertain of his next move.

A brief whistle drew the lad nearer. 'You wanted to speak to me, mister?'

'How would you like to earn yourself four bits, son?'

At once the turned-down mouth quirked into a pleasant grin. 'I guess it depends on what you want done for your money,' he replied cautiously.

'Four bits, payable in advance. All I want you to do is take a little message down the street.' He waited until a stroller had gone by and was out of earshot, 'Tell Carlos Fuente, the deputy, that Marshal O'Halloran would like to speak to him right away in the cafe. Tell him it is urgent. That's all. Think you can do that?'

The lad did a cartwheel in very little space, ran the half dollar piece up his bare arm like a conjurer and danced off up the boards to carry out his assignment. Drifter then dodged back across the street and made tracks in the same direction. Whenever the boy paused, he made sure that he was out of sight. Fortunately, there were plenty of parked vehicles on the south side of the street.

The tension mounted in the Texan as the boy disappeared into the office. The minute before Fuente came out dragged like five. Eventually, the deputy stopped fidgeting with his undented hat and shuffled off up the sidewalk on his short legs. His own eating time was near. He did not like any special duties at a time like this.

The boy did another couple of cartwheels. He whistled after Carlos, failed to gain his attention and eventually set off up the street in the other direction. Two strollers, one going each way both idled their way past the peace office. They glanced in through the window without paying too much attention and moved on again.

Drifter dropped to the dirt of the street, his attention never keener.

Fifteen paces and he was up on the sidewalk opposite. Several tiny doubts went through his mind. What if the sorrel had broken loose and gone for a walk? Supposing someone in his brief absence had noted that the bank robber's horse was freshly saddled? He knocked on the door, although he did not expect any answer, and stepped inside almost at once.

To his surprise, the office was not deserted. A hard-eyed veteran with a white waxed moustache came out of the marshal's chair with a guilty look on his deeply lined features and pointed the shotgun which he had been cleaning approximately in the direction of the visitor.

Drifter hoped his face did not betray his amazement, 'Er, howdy. I wanted to have a word with the marshal before leavin' town. Did I pick a bad time to call?'

The red-faced man grinned, showing chipped brown teeth. 'If you wanted to see him in a hurry you couldn't have picked a worse time. He's along the street havin' his dinner. Worse still, he's jest sent a message for Fuente to go and talk to him. Me, I'm only the constable around here. Don't think I could do anything to help you. I could give him a message, I suppose, if you're on the point of leavin'?'

The constable was not really keen to be bothered. Interest was already flickering out of his weathered face when Drifter managed a reply.

'Don't bother about the message, amigo. I'll slip along to the cafe an' talk to him. Sorry to have disturbed you. Adios.'

Drifter backed out into the street, temporarily frustrated and baffled. He could hardly step back into the office with a mask over his face and point a gun at the old-timer cleaning the weapons. After all, one or other of them was liable to get hurt. He nibbled his lip, disgusted with himself for not having known that another man was around the place. His original plan had been to grab the keys in the deserted office, open Lopez's cell door and then take his cousin out by the back entrance in the end of the cell block.

That would have to be changed. He started to think about an alternative plan. There were cracks in the adobe walling underneath the grille in Lopez's cell. With two mounts, did he have sufficient horse power to pull the grille out of the wall?

If he tried and failed, the noise involved would raise the alarm. He would have to toss in a weapon and leave it to Lopez to get the drop on the constable and force his way out of doors.

He took the shortest route back to Second Street, running a few steps from time to time without being aware of it. His shirt was sticking to his chest by the time he trotted back over the familiar territory and paused by the cell block wall.

'Lopez! A change of plan. I'm goin' to have to try an' pull away the grille.

Stand by for a pistol, in case we're interrupted.'

The prisoner caught the weapon on its way to the floor, inside the cell. He whispered: 'What happened, cousin? Did that old timer in the front office frighten you?'

Drifter ignored him. 'Fasten this loop to the bars. I'll be back with another.'

In the anxiety he had forgotten to bring along his own sorrel, which would now be needed. He remedied his error, and soon a second lariat was attached to the bars. Controlling the horses side by side, with the roan nearer the cell wall, he filled his lungs with air and steeled himself for the crucial effort which would be required. The horses had to provide the power, but the controlling of them would be no mean task.

He started to urge them to a greater effort. The sorrel responded first, its hauling swinging it into the roan which sidefooted and complained. He whacked the rump of the riderless horse with his reins and lightly rowelled the sorrel. The horses collided again, but this time they were both pulling hard and seeking to outdo one another.

The crack in the wall extended in all directions. Lopez, standing on his bench, heaved. Just as the combined effort was waning, the section of wall with the grille in its centre creaked and swung outwards. Lopez roared as his body was hauled through with it. Upwards of a foot of adobe beneath the spot where the grille had been fell out into the open air, bouncing on the ground and sending up a cloud of powdery dust and grit.

Lopez, who was jarring his wrists, let go. He did a forward roll, came up off his shoulder and lunged for his roan, at the same time frantically clawing for his stetson which wanted to part company.

In the office, the constable yelled out something unintelligible, partly in anger and partly in surprise. Lopez ripped away the end of the lariat from the saddle horn. He removed his revolver from his waistband for greater readiness and lunged up into the saddle.

Drifter, ahead of him and already freed from the lariat, called out: 'Follow me! Don't shoot unless you have to! No heroics on the way. I've worked out a detour before we head south!'

On the way through the passage, the roan was close behind the sorrel. A single rifle bullet flew over their heads as they erupted into the street, but they did not panic. Drifter headed west at a fair lick. Some fifty yards further on, he turned into a cross passage which led into Third Street.

Meanwhile, the frantic constable was firing his shotgun into the air to attract the maximum of attention.

Drifter dismounted. Lopez did the same. They moved closer, as though heading for the livery up the end of the street. When most eyes were off them, the Texan headed back into an alley and crossed vacant lots going south.

Some three or four minutes elapsed before the first mounted men headed north in the wake of the prisoner and his liberator. By that time, they were just crossing Main Street with their mounts masking their faces. Still moving leisurely, they crossed over into the Mexican section and did not mount up again until they had crossed a small stream used for washing purposes.

In the first belt of trees south of town they hit leather and started to go with a vengeance. Some thirty minutes later, they slowed down, but all through the rest of the afternoon they pushed their labouring mounts at a good pace.

The need to make distance killed what might have been a relatively pleasant reunion. As it was, fears of pursuit kept them silent and tense by the hour. They took their first rest around seven in the evening, riding for almost three hundred yards into scrub-land before unsaddling.

Over a low fire, they prepared a scratch meal. Lopez's wolfish expression became more human when he noted the quality of the victuals.

'You did all right in your shoppin', cousin.'

Drifter paused long enough in his chores to grin at him. 'I did the shoppin' but the treat is on you, cousin.' He fished from his shirt a bundle of notes amounting to four hundred dollars and tossed them over. 'That's your share of the reward money.'

Lopez caught the bundle with ease. Admiration showed briefly in his face. 'Doggone it, you caught up with those two rascals, Graft an' Marvin. How did you make out?'

Most of the explaining was done at the same time as food was being chewed. For a short while the atmosphere between them was cordial. Soon, however, they were back at verbal sniping. Drifter cut it short by insisting on getting back to the trail and making greater distance before nightfall.

They made another ten miles before finally camping down for the night. When they were wrapped up in their blankets. Drifter had important things to say.

'While we were separated this time, I had a lot of conjecturin' to do. I don't know now whether we ought to pursue loot that has been stolen from a church. But we'll give it a go. If we don't catch up with it, we either part company or we try to earn an honest livin'.'

Drifter spoke with an air of finality. Lopez heard him well and wondered if he was right. He offered no sort of argument about the possible change of plans. Drifter was the first asleep.

* * *

The next day they resumed the ride. The pace was slower. They were more watchful, getting off the track to avoid curious travellers going north who could identify them to any pursuers. In the afternoon, they identified and passed the spot where Drifter had helped get the wagon back on the trail. Gradually, the broiling sun sapped their vitality and their will to make progress. Their mounts slowed appreciably and the old doubts about their partnership and their way of life began to irritate them all over again.

By the time they were willing to make camp, at a spot considerably nearer that great boundary marker, the Rio Grande river, they were not far from exhaustion. In addition, their tempers were near to flashpoint.

13

Not many days had elapsed since the time when Lopez and subsequently Drifter had made their contacts with the family of wagoners know as the Carreras. For all parties, however, the interval of time had seemed longer.

At the time when Drifter and Lopez were bedding down wide of the trail leading south to the Rio Grande and Mexico, the crew of the wagon were also preparing for the night less than ten miles away. In direction, the Carreras' camp was south-east of the other, smaller one. If they had stayed on the main track heading for the great river, the direction would have been nearer south: but they had left it. Ernesto and Joseph had put their heads together the day before and decided that too many small time bandits were playing upon isolated units of travellers on the trail proper.

A man travelling the opposite way had been grateful for a meal offered to him. By way of recompense he had pointed out certain landmarks which led to a prudent travellers' loop. An alternative route, looping away from the main one, which enabled knowing travellers to diverge from the regular track for several miles which were the most tricky in regard to being attacked.

Consequently, the Carreras' wagon was drawn up on a useful patch of tufted grass on the eastern side of a pair of spine-backed ridges which separated them from the main trail.

Since the visit of the horse riding cousins, one after the other, only modest progress had been made by the family towards the border and their home on the other side. On this particular night, young Cipriana, perhaps more than the other, older people was feeling rather tired and out of sorts with herself. The mission of the family and Father Joseph appeared to have failed. They would have to return to their old home town, Cuidad Nuevo, and try to resume life where they had left off. The very thought of a return to the town without any sort of success made her shudder.

It was no longer a happy place. In fact, travellers calling briefly often referred to it these days as Cuidad Perdido, 'Lost Town,' or 'Town of the Lost.' For two years it had been like that, and now it seemed that the failure of Father Joseph's efforts in the United States would mean a longer period of poverty and unhappiness for those original townspeople who still stayed on.

As she thought these thoughts, Cipriana was seated on a low stool in the back of the wagon combing her long copper-coloured hair. An hour or more earlier she had washed her tresses in a clear pool, and now it sparkled like thin strands of copper wire. But who was to see it? Lopez had not returned: neither had his tall Texan cousin, Drifter.

Joseph offered her polite compliments in his own special way, but that did not seem to count with the girl. She sighed, yawned, and wondered what she could do to alter her appearance.

Some fifteen minutes earlier, she had finished the chores occasioned by the evening meal. As soon as the pots and pans were cleaned Alicia had seated herself on a rock quite close to the fire. Restlessness stopped Cipriana from doing the same. On one occasion, Ernesto had called to her, requesting her to return to the fire and sing for them, to the music of Joseph's guitar. She had replied with an evasive answer. At once, her father and mother had raised their voices in a slight quarrel over her. Joseph, as frequently happened, had been the one to heal the breach. He had suggested that she wanted to be alone with her thoughts.

By way of recompense, he sang in his rich baritone voice while his agile fingers conjured songs out of the stringed instrument.

The wagon rocked ever so slightly as the girl shifted her position on the stool. At the same time, the lamp swinging from overhead moved through a slight arc casting flickering shadows this way and that in a regular moving pattern.

With one hand, she scooped together her long tresses and held them at the nape of her neck. Next, she trailed the tail of her hair over her left shoulder, and finally she allowed it all to swing free and cascade round her neck and shoulders like a great bell. The swinging lamp added radiance to the lustre in her hair. She found herself wishing that Drifter was nearer to witness it. But that was out of the question. Wishful thinking. He had ridden north after his restless cousin and there was no sort of reason why he should ever come back this way.

For a few seconds, she glanced away, seeing in her mind's eye instead the full handsome face of Drifter framed with the auburn sideburns and the closely-trimmed beard. There was that special quality in the green eyes. Firmness in the lines of his face. His willingness to help others in difficulty. At the time, she knew Father Joseph had been much impressed by him. She wondered how Joseph would react if he knew the remarkable effect Drifter's presence had upon her. With a woman, of course, it was different. Different again with her. She had long since acknowledged to herself that she longed for his return, not just as a casual acquaintance, but as a figure to remain permanently in her life; to enrich it as her father had done her mother's many years ago.

As she mused and glanced back in the mirror at herself, it occurred to her that she had done no dressing up worthy of mention for rather a long time. On this protracted journey, mostly she had been dressed in peasant blouses and short riding skirts. In her travelling trunk she had long skirts, a dress or two, more dressy blouses and many other items of a more intimate nature.

Somewhere in the bottom of the box was a set of three pieces: a necklace, a ring and a bracelet. They had been given her for her twenty-first birthday by her parents. The trinkets were fashioned out of gold and decorated with the rather pleasant stone known as Mexican onyx.

She glanced out through the forward end of the wagon, saw that the other three were fully wrapped up in each other, and decided to get out the jewels and try them on. In moving over to the travelling box, her moccasined feet caused the base boards to creek. Joseph's profile under the broad Quaker-style hat shifted as he glanced in her direction. He kept on singing, however, and no one remarked about what she was doing.

Peering down through the screen of her hair, she fumbled with the leather fastenings. With one still to go, she attempted to move the trunk a few inches to one side, so that the lamp would shine directly into it when it was opened. It was heavier than she remembered. A minute later, she had the lid up and met with a big surprise. Inside her trunk, resting squarely upon clothing which she had hoped to keep free of creases until they were back home again, was a smaller trunk. She had never seen it before. It was of heavy, seamed leather, much knocked about, and with its hasp held in place by a split pin.

Two or three minutes of struggle were sufficient for her to exhaust herself in the effort of opening it. It was too much for her. Breathing hard, she moved lightly towards the front end of the wagon, where she paused with her hands on her hips and looked down on the features of the others, indistinctly seen in the flickering light from the fire.

Joseph's playing came to an end. He was aware of her movements, and his awareness spread to her parents. Once again, Alicia begged her to join them and sing before turning in. The girl ignored them, instead declaring her find.

'In my travellin' trunk there's a smaller trunk I've never seen anywhere before. Seamed black leather, it has, an' it's quite heavy. Does anyone claim it?'

The new topic of conversation had the effect of rousing the other three members of the party. It was established almost at once that none of them had such a trunk. Such was the curiosity that the two men climbed into the wagon and dragged the strange trunk out into the open, dumping it on the ground by the fire.

Cipriana pranced along behind them, holding the lamp. With a knife, Joseph extracted the holding pin. Ernesto opened the lid and pulled back the square of silk cloth which hid the contents. All four heads craned forward to see what mysteries were within. None were disappointed. Uppermost was a gold crucifix about eighteen inches in length, studded with lustrous stones which caught the firelight as soon as it was removed in Joseph's capable hands.

'Holy father,' Ernesto murmured ecstatically, while the others gasped at the sheer beauty of the piece.

Joseph placed the cross upon the ground, laying it on the silk found in the box. Next, he brought out a golden chalice, and while Alicia's soft hands were going over it he drew out the rolled painting of the mother and child.

'Every night this week I have been praying for guidance in recovering the lost relics of the church of our town. It is hard to believe that Cuidad Perdido will get back its precious pieces, but it seems that they are back in our hands.'

'Tell me, Father Joseph,' Alicia begged, 'is this some sort of miracle?'

Cipriana, perhaps the last to recover from the shock of finding the precious items, moved swiftly to her mother and comforted her.

'For those who believe,' Joseph replied, 'this has to be a miracle of sorts. Even though we may discover how the trunk came to be left in our wagon.'

His steady eyes turned in the direction of the girl, whose thoughts at once went back to the cousins' visits.

Ernesto was saying: 'If we wanted proof, this madonna and child is all we need. Alicia an' me, we remember it being on the wall of the church ever since our marriage.'

'It is true. This painting was on the wall all the time my brother was priest of Cuidad Nuevo,' Joseph murmured.

Alicia crossed herself. 'Si. Before El Mestizo sacked the village an' robbed the church, leaving your brother near to death. When the precious relics are restored, the people of the town will have their faith restored. They will no longer think of Cuidad Nuevo as Cuidad Perdido.'

'But how did this miracle come about? How did we receive the trunk? Has it been there for a long time?'

'Either Lopez or Drifter put it there,' Cipriana explained confidently. 'But I don't think Drifter would have had the time. So it must have been his cousin.'

She was thinking that Lopez would come back for it, but she did not like to think of such a thing. Especially as it was possible for Drifter to come back with him. What did this miracle mean in the lives of the trail-riding cousins?

Clearly, Ernesto and Alicia were also having doubts. Joseph refilled the coffee pot and seated himself to try and explain.

'I believe that box to be the property of El Mestizo, himself, the border bandit. The man who was reported as killed in a border incident miles west of here. There is much money in the bottom of the trunk. Thousands of dollars in big notes.'

Ernesto mopped perspiration from his jowl. 'But if that is so, then our friend, Lopez, must have taken it from the bandido. Does not that make Lopez as much of an undesirable character as El Mestizo himself?'

Cipriana's thoughts had travelled that far. She wanted to emit the word 'No,' but she only managed to gasp, which Joseph correctly interpreted.

Alicia, more forthright, remarked: 'He deserves to die for trading in relics of our church. If he carried these for his personal gain, he will return! And you two men will know what to do when he gets here!'

Again Cipriana wanted to call out in the negative. This time she restrained herself altogether.

'You mean we should shoot him? Maybe both of them?' Ernesto queried. He turned to Joseph. 'Do you believe that they will come back again for the box? Will you give it to them?'

The cleric was slow to answer. 'I will not easily give up the precious belongings of the church which my brother died in trying to protect. After all, the search for them was all that drew us north of the border. I believe that possibly Lopez came upon the box accidentally. I would not shoot him out of hand. Unintentionally, he has done us a service by leaving the box with us. We would be uncharitable if we did not give him a chance to explain about them.'

'And Drifter will have things to say,' Cipriana added. 'I cannot think that Drifter would wish to profit by our church's losses. But the more I think of these things, the more certain I am that the riders will come back. Perhaps at daybreak, we ought to keep a lookout for them instead of hurrying back to the great river.'

'Tonight, Cipriana's lips achieve wisdom beyond her years,' Joseph commented warmly. 'It is time to turn in. We must be long at our prayers this night. Tomorrow Ernesto and I must be awake early. We may have to ride back to the main trail in search of our young riding friends who may be back this way.'

Joseph secured the trunk with a lariat through the handle before dropping off to sleep beside the fire in the company of Ernesto. Cipriana, sharing the wagon with her mother, offered up her prayers in silence.

In content, they differed quite considerably from those of her parents. Her prayers had two main points in them. Firstly, that Drifter and Lopez would soon return, and, secondly, if it was proved that the cousins were acting after the fashion of outlaws, that they would be found to be only mildly dishonest.

14

The office of Jake Kilbride in Laredo received the telegraph message from Mark Denver in Rio City on that same day as the banker met with the lawyer and town marshal. Consequently, Kilbride and his two riding associates, Sam and Henry Block, were able to leave Laredo almost at once. Denver had promised a generous deal for a few days' work, and Kilbride, an ex-Pinkerton detective, had at once thrown all his resources into the Denver case. In fact, the three riders entered Rio just a short while after Drifter had brought about the rescue of his cousin.

O'Halloran and Fuente were nearly frantic, due to the pressure being put upon them by the banker. As soon as the banker started to tongue-lash the tired newcomers, Kilbride took his men off to the Border saloon where they began to take the dryness out of their throats with beer and whiskey.

Kilbride was a stocky, aggressive character in his late forties, slightly above average height and dressed in a black stetson and a tailored brown suit. His skin was sallow, his eyes very dark. A neat black moustache practically hid his firm mouth.

His cousins, the Block brothers, were younger and far from looking alike in appearance. Sam in his early thirties and a former army corporal, was tall, full-faced and fresh-complexioned. Henry was twenty-six. He was three inches shorter and possessed a very full shaven jaw and underlip. His hair was thick, brown, curly and springy. Each of the Blocks wore a grey stores suit and a derby hat. Only their twin guns gave any sort of inkling as to their job in life. The Kilbride Agency was supposed to be a detective outfit, but it was known to take on many other assignments other than investigations.

Their arrival in Rio was an anti-climax after the departure of the bank robber and his partner. In allowing a little time to pass before doing anything about the chase, Kilbride was able to sift through two or three stories about the direction which the runaways had taken.

The delay also had the effect of making Banker Denver raise his rate for the job of recovering a certain box and eliminating the opposition afterwards. Kilbride spent a half hour in the private office of the bank ironing out one or two basic differences between his own and the banker's thinking on the matter of this difficult case. When he was assured that the interests of himself and his associates would be taken care of to the full, he then made rapid preparations to ride off towards the south.

On fresh horses, the trio were not so very far behind the fugitives on that first night out of town. No more than five miles separated the two camps during the quiet hours. Drifter and Lopez, however, were the first to be up and about the next morning and they had done a few more miles in the southerly direction before Kilbride's outfit was up and under way.

Oddly enough, the two fugitives did not notice the turn-off onto the secondary track which was the safety loop for small parties going south. But they were on the alert to other things. A brief encounter with a band of trailside thieves who preyed upon travellers had the effect of changing their plans.

The thieves accepted them as more of their own kind and when they asked questions about a certain covered wagon with four occupants they were told that no wagon answering that description had gone through in the past couple of days.

As a direct result of this conversation. Drifter and Lopez had turned back on their tracks and were riding north again, studiously looking for a sidetrack on the eastern aspect of the main trail. It was barely nine o'clock when they neared the hidden fork, preceded by others.

★ ★ ★

Kilbride and his partners, better informed about local detail had reined in some fifty yards from the spot where a stand of stunted oak trees masked the beginning of the loop track.

'So what do we do now? A fork is a fork, but we can't take both routes. An' sign don't show itself on this sort of rocky track well enough to be sure which direction they took.'

Kilbride ignored his cousin for a while, mopping his neck and studying the land round about them. The runaways could have gone on, straight for the river and the border, or they could have turned off on the lesser trail. It all depended where in the first place the box of missing loot had been hidden.

Sam roughly rocked his saddle. His younger brother slightly the more patient, used his spyglass to good effect. He clicked his tongue and snapped the glass shut while his brother tried to read his face and Kilbride glowered at him.

'No need to cudgel that brain of yours, cousin,' Henry remarked lightly, ''cause the two hombres we're lookin' for are comin' up from the south right now. At least, I guess it's them. The joker with the steeple hat sure looks a whole lot like the man on the reward notice, an' the big fellow with the auburn hair sounds a whole lot like that there constable's description of him. So where do we go to earth?'

Sam muttered: 'If you're mistaken about this, little brother, I'm goin' to pin your ears back.'

Kilbride felt like cutting his youngest partner down to size, but he knew of the excellence of Henry's eyesight and so he said nothing, at first.

'I reckon we'll go to ground on the west side. Behind the trailside rocks an' scrub will do. Leave me to take the lead. And remember we ain't aimin' to eliminate anyone at this stage. Cripple them, if need be, but make sure they're still able to talk.'

The Block boys nodded in agreement, and headed for the west side taking their mounts with them. At the same time, Ernesto Carreras and Father Joseph scrambled to a vantage point which overlooked the main trail at the point of intersection. Leading the brown mare and a youthful shaft horse, they headed into a nest of rocks jutting out like a natural balcony one hundred and fifty feet above trail level on the nearer of the two spine-backed ridges.

* * *

Father Joseph remarked: 'Ernesto, I believe we are just in time. Here come our friends right now. Up the trail from the south. And three other men who have jest spotted them are hurrying into trailside rocks on the other side of the trail. We are due for an ambush.'

Ernesto, who was many pounds overweight, was gasping for breath when he reached the vantage point. He stared into Joseph's face almost unbelievingly. While he still laboured to recover his breath, the younger man put his rifle to his shoulder and worked a shell into the breech.

'Sometimes I think you are in direct communication with the Almighty,' Ernesto murmured. 'How could you know that as soon as we reached the top of this ridge that Drifter an' Lopez would ride into sight?'

'Don't be foolish, amigo,' Joseph chided him, 'I didn't know. It seemed a good thing to do to seek a vantage point. That was all. Now hurry. We must take steps to make sure our acquaintances are not hurt. I don't think those who search for them want them dead, yet. But they would be better in our hands than in those of strangers.'

'If we are goin' to fire on the other three, shall we not put ourselves beyond the law? Are they not peace officers?'

'I don't think so. They were not wearing badges. We shall have to use our weapons even if only to scare off the ambushers.'

★ ★ ★

Drifter and Lopez came up slowly, almost as if they were in slow motion. Joseph gave a sharp intake of breath. Almost at once, a single rifle fired from the rocks on the west side. The bullet flew in front of the mount of Drifter, who was just ahead of his cousin.

The sorrel reared up, but was swiftly brought under control. Lopez yelled in anger and turned his attention to his left, the direction from which the bullet had come. Drifter called out something which did not carry to the ridge. Instantly, both fugitives flattened themselves along their horses necks and applied their spurs.

This acted like a signal for the ambushers to increase their fire power.

Lopez's legs were tightly wrapped round the barrel of the roan. His spurs really dug in. The low barrelled animal increased its speed and might have galloped into the sorrel had not Drifter suddenly turned it off-trail towards the east, heading for rock cover on the side away from the attack, Lopez went ahead, and then copied his partner's manoeuvre. Other bullets came from the same cluster of rocks, but all of them were ahead of the riders. Kilbride was thinking in terms of shouting a challenge as soon as the riders reached cover. The unexpected prevented him.

The two rifles up on the ridge fired almost as one. They were aimed to hit the rocks behind which the ambushers were crouching. Both richocheted, diverted by the rocks which they hit. The noises they made affected the ambushers' nerves. Other shots followed, making Kilbride and his boys duck down low to avoid the splinters of stone and the flying lead.

By the time a dozen bullets had flown

in their direction, the two startled horsemen had disappeared from view, along with their mounts. Drifter and Lopez, doubly startled, threw themselves out of leather, taking their shoulder guns with them and prepared to return the hostile fire.

For a few minutes, bullets flew from east to west, fired at two levels. They did not desist at either level until it was perceived by Joseph and Ernesto that the ambushers were pulling out.

Kilbride and the Block boys had decided that discretion was the better part of valour. Assailed from two directions, they withdrew towards the west and kept on going. A brief span of time elapsed before Drifter and Lopez desisted. They were both angered by the sudden assault, although they ought to have been prepared for hostile action ever since they quit Rio.

'Ho, down there! You two know who it is helpin' you?'

The voice of Ernesto was immediately identified. Lopez called back. 'Is that you, Ernesto? You couldn't have turned up at a more useful time!'

The two down in the rocks stood up and waved. Joseph waved back at them. He called: 'We were expecting a visit from you, an' we thought you might possibly run into trouble! Work your way round the foot of the ridge! Our wagon is round the back!'

As they moved back into leather, the cousins exchanged a few startled words. 'Who'd have thought it,' Drifter muttered, 'the very same folk we've failed to find come to our rescue.'

Lopez laughed dryly. 'Sure, an' how should they know we could be in trouble? Unless they know why we're lookin' for them.'

The two pairs came together ten minutes later. There was a lot of warm handshaking before they moved on down the loop track, on the way to where the Carreras' covered wagon was parked. After a few cordial enquiries had been exchanged, there was a short pause. Drifter broke the silence.

'Unknown to me when I visited you before, Lopez left a box in your wagon. Or so he tells me.'

Lopez sniffed and lowered his eyes. He was riding on the outside of the two men from the wagon. 'It is true. When I first met up with you, I had left it behind. But in the night, I slipped away from the camp and recovered it, leavin' it inside one of the bigger trunks.'

Ernesto shot a troubled glance in the direction of Father Joseph. The latter nodded and turned his attention particularly to Lopez.

'Señor Lopez, I have to tell you that we found your trunk last night. Not knowing anything about it, we opened it and were very surprised by its contents.'

Ernesto was studying the reactions of the cousins very closely. All he could be sure of, however, was embarrassment.

Drifter said: 'I think you must have found precious items in gold, although I have never seen them myself.'

'Yes, indeed,' Joseph admitted. 'A

crucifix, a chalice, a painting of the madonna and child, and a great deal of money. The items other than the money were all stolen from the church of a small Mexican settlement which was known as Cuidad Nuevo.

'My brother was the priest. He lost his life in trying to safeguard them from El Mestizo, the border bandit. These days, people call the village Cuidad Perdido. I myself am the new priest. I crossed into the United States especially to try and trace the stolen relics. Remarkable circumstances have returned them into my hands.'

Drifter and Lopez both studiously avoided the eyes of their friends.

'And what do you think of my cousin and I now, Father Joseph?' Drifter asked tensely.

'I think you have fallen into bad ways, that you have lived by stealing. But I do not believe you would rob a church. Am I right?'

'You are right about our bein' thieves. We would not rob a church.

Those relics came into my cousin's possession purely by accident. For my part, I want nothing to do with them.'

'Neither do I,' Lopez added, in a small voice.

'Then there is still the possibility of friendship between us,' Joseph decided.

Ernesto visibly relaxed. Lopez remained silent, his mind in a turmoil. Uppermost in Drifter's thoughts was the sort of reception they would get from the women when they reached the wagon.

15

Long before the wagon was reached, a profitable discussion took place between the two parties. It was decided beyond the reasonable doubt of any of them that El Mestizo's treasure, stolen from the bank, had more or less become the property of Denver, the bank manager and, that in seeking to recover it, he wanted it back for his own purposes.

Alicia was slow to come forward when she heard the sound of horses, but Cipriana knew no such restraint. She ran forward in her mocassins beaming with pleasure, long before it was ascertained by the older woman that Father Joseph was still on quite friendly terms with the cousins. The priest was quick to explain.

'Our friends don't object to our taking the church treasures back to our town. In fact, Drifter, here, was just offering himself and his cousin as an escort of guards, in the event that those who recently lost the box come again looking for it.'

'Good, good. I am pleased,' Alicia remarked, with obvious relief. 'But now, do you want food?'

'We need to move on, wife. Three men back there on the main trail were about to ambush our friends. We may have more trouble very soon.'

Food was postponed, and the whole outfit got under way within ten minutes. Ernesto's words, however, were to prove prophetic.

★ ★ ★

Two days later, after keeping themselves apart from others on all possible occasions, the wagon, the wagoners and the riders were rafting across an infrequently used part of the Rio Grande. The time was towards midday. No one else was using the raft at the time, although it was there for the use of anyone. Two long thick manilla ropes stretched from bank to bank assisted with the steering. Some two hundred yards clear of the northern bank (and the United States) Drifter and Lopez were assisting a smooth passage by throwing their combined weight upon the stern oar.

Lopez was muttering: 'I would like to know what will happen to the fifty thousand dollars in the bottom of the loot box. Me, I will sell my services as a guard an' guide very dearly.'

'Don't go spoilin' things by actin' mean at this stage, cousin,' Drifter panted, 'we have decent honest folks for friends, for the first time in years. Besides, we're lucky to clear the States ahead of Denver.'

Before the Texican could answer a long ranging rifle shot came from the northern bank passing over the raft and startling everyone upon it. Joseph urged all the family round the other side of the wagon, while Cipriana called back to the stern oarsmen.

'Sam! Manuel! Come away from there! You could be shot! Look at the bunched horsemen on the bank! They are your enemies!'

During their travels, she had elicited the cousins' family name, which was Woolley. Drifter, of course, answered to Sam, while his cousin was christened Manuel. Drifter waved to her, but he muttered fiercely under his breath.

'That's Denver again. *And* his town marshal! They are no hired bank guards. If you ask me, they'll come across the river after us, they're so keen now to get the loot back.'

'Yes, some hombre has the glass on us. They could have recognised our horses. We shouldn't have left them at the back of the raft. As soon as we get across, we'll have to take avoidin' action.'

Reluctantly, the partners abandoned the stern oar and moved forward to comparative safety. Other bullets flew at them from riflemen on foot. Upwards of a score of men were bunched on the bank. Kilbride and the Block brothers were in the party.

Presently, the shooting, which was ineffective, faded out. Instead Denver's men hacked through the steering ropes in an attempt to hinder the crossing of the raft. To counter this new threat. Drifter and his cousin returned to the stern oar and kept up the forward progress.

On the north bank, Denver sent riders to east and west to search out a fordable part of the river within easy riding distance.

The cousins, who had often made the crossing not far ahead of trouble, knew that no such fords existed near at hand. Sooner or later, the pursuers would become aware of this.

Joseph came aft to talk with the oarsmen. His face showed his concern, which he had been anxious to hide from the Carreras family.

'Tell me, Drifter, do you think the posse will cross the river, even though it means crossing into foreign territory outside the control of the United States?'

Drifter gave a wry grin. 'By this time, that banker is so keen on recoverin' the treasure nothin' will stop him. They'll cross, all right, an' they may not be far behind us. How far is it to Cuidad Perdido?'

'A few hours drive almost due south. I very much doubt if we could keep ahead of them, unless something can be done to put them on the wrong track. I fear for the lives of the Carreras as much as for the relics. What do you think can be done?'

Lopez, whose face was dripping with perspiration, cocked an eyebrow at Drifter, who tried to look confident. 'We two will have to lure them away from the direct route to the town. There's a divergin' track goes further west, not far up the bank. If we do a good job an' manage to steer clear of the *rurales* all could go well for us. I take it you will be safe if you are still ahead by the time the town is reached?'

Joseph favoured them with a frank look from his searching blue eyes. After drawing out the sweatband of his Quaker-style hat, he slowly shook his head.

'Even then, I cannot be sure. The adobes form a wide square around the church. Many of the original townsfolk have moved away since the troubles. Those who remain are living in the houses to the south and west. The evacuated adobes have in places been taken over by undesirables. Men of both races on the run from the police of Mexico and the United States. If I manage to get through to the church then the faithful may rally and drive out the outlaws.'

'So there's likely to be some fighting, even if we get there without incident,' Drifter remarked, breathing hard.

'*If* we ever get there,' Lopez added cynically.

Father Joseph spread his hands in a gesture of resignation. 'We are in the hands of the Almighty. I can only thank you for what you have done already, and hope that you are still with us.'

Before either of the oarsmen could answer the front end of the raft scraped the Mexican bank and all of them were thrown forward with a jerk. Joseph hurried to the other end of the raft to assist Ernesto with the lead horses. Cipriana glanced back at the cousins, at the same time helping Alicia, her mother, to mount the box.

At first, the horses' shoes slithered on the soft soil of the bank. As the minutes slipped away, and the signs on the northern bank showed at least one reconnaissance party returning to the spot opposite them, Drifter's nerves began to play up.

'Leave the oar, cousin,' he called hoarsely, 'Help me to push the cart!'

Muttering oaths unfit for mixed company, Lopez grudgingly agreed to help. There was a lot of shouting and urging before the lead horses got a purchase on the mud. After that it was only a matter of keeping the team going. The front end of the wagon rocked. Alicia called out sharply in alarm. Fortunately, it did not tilt far enough to turn over.

The cousins stopped pushing when it was twenty yards clear. They stood with their shoulders hunched, breathing hard and knowing great tiredness. Joseph and Ernesto stayed at the rear for a few yards more while the two ill-assorted escorts went back for their horses and hastily mounted up.

Some fifty yards above the bank, a solid rank of willows and other lush trees of the area encroached upon the track, shortly before it forked. The wagon closely followed by the riders, kept going until they were out of sight from the river and then stopped for a last consultation.

Ernesto mounted to the box, while Joseph stood breathless with his hands on his hips. 'I'll take the wagon off-trail for a few yards so as not to show an immediate trail. Will that help?'

'It will help, Father,' Drifter remarked

firmly. 'Now, get going, an' if you are overtaken don't give up the box without a fight. They can only guess that you have it. It's still Lopez and me they're after. Good luck. If all goes well, we'll join you in town.'

Joseph shook hands with them both. 'Go with God, my friends,' he remarked warmly.

And then Ernesto was swinging the team around to make a detour. Shouting farewell cries, the mounted riders pulled away and went off down the fork which headed west. Not far along it Drifter swung off into the trees and headed back for the river.

'Are you mad, cousin? Hell an' tarnation, you're ridin' straight back into trouble!'

'Maybe I am,' Drifter conceded, 'but keepin' the posse away from the wagon won't be easy! Stay with me an' let's see if we can stir things up a bit.'

'I'm not happy with that treasure box out of my sight,' Lopez admitted, but he too turned off and began a cautious ride downhill through trees, the branches of which threatened to remove them from the saddle at any unguarded moment.

When they were close enough to see across the great river, the first half dozen riders were plunging into the water, their mounts kicking up spray in the faces of others. The partners dismounted, and fired off half a dozen rounds apiece from the shelter of tree boles. Two swimming horses panicked and tipped their riders into the water, but the others merely spread out and came on apace.

A scattering of shots came back at them, but no damage was done either way. As the swimmers came nearer, Drifter stepped clear of his tree bole and allowed them to get a good look at him. Lopez, who believed in doing things in style, waved his steeple hat and called them a lot of dirty gringos, and other, less pleasant things.

Soon, the partners were mounted again and working hard to get back on their track. They made good progress as soon as they were on it and fired off a couple of revolver shots to make sure that the posse kept on their heels.

Denver and his men made a good job of the pursuit. After an hour the partners emerged on a southern slope clear of trees and reined in for a short rest. Within five minutes they became aware of another hazard. A bunch of a dozen *rurales* were grouped around a small fire not more than four hundred yards away to westward and within a stone's throw of the west trail.

The two groups spotted each other at the same time.

'Now what do we do?' Drifter asked anxiously.

'We avoid the Mexican police at all costs. They are far trickier than our pursuers. They are crafty enough to take us into custody an' auction us off to the banker and his men. There is only one course open to us, cousin. Me, I don't like hostile groups on two sides.'

'So we cut off down this slope and head directly for Cuidad Perdido,'

Drifter opined. 'Before Denver notices our change of plan. Here's hoping we don't heap more troubles on the heads of Joseph and his friends.'

So saying, he put the sorrel at the slope, ignoring the cries of the *rurales*, muted by distance.

16

The descent onto lower ground for anyone riding at speed was precipitous and highly dangerous. Both Drifter and Lopez were inclined to recklessness in the first few minutes after the *rurales* had fired a couple of warning shots in their direction.

Fortunately, the horses reacted well to the sudden challenge. The riders were jolted this way and that in their saddles, but no mishaps occurred. The Mexicans were soon out of sight, due to the fact that they had to tighten their saddle girths before starting the pursuit.

Consequently, the partners slowed down after a while and began to think about their present plight. As they came out of the lower ground and pointed their horses on a converging course with the trail taken by the wagon, they were anything but confident.

'We are fools, amigo,' Lopez insisted. 'We had a fortune in our hands an' we have allowed ourselves to be diverted by a single priest with a prior claim. He could have had his baubles, but what about that wad of money underneath them?

'Fifty thousand dollars is a lot of money. If the posse catches up with us before we get to the town, we could spend a long time in an American jail instead of puttin' our feet up an' livin' well. Tell me I'm wrong, if you can, cousin.'

'It's true we have turned our backs on a fortune, but I think we shall make it to Perdido, an' that the priest will give us a useful reward. So let's shake the *rurales* off our back trail an' keep a sharp lookout for the posse. We've been on the run before an' ridden clear of trouble.'

Drifter was thinking about Cipriana, but he did not use her in his argument about going on and honouring their pledge to distract the American posse. He thought that his cousin would only mock him. He was sure for the first time of a serious divergence in their views.

In order to keep up a reasonable speed, the riders jogged along a well grassed patch of open ground just clear of the timbered southern slope. From time to time, one or other of them stood up in the stirrups to take a good look around.

After ten minutes, Lopez spotted the first of the *rurales* emerging from the comparative shade of the trees. The man in question, a rotund fellow with a long drooping moustache, pointed after them. Chuckling to himself, the Texican waved to him and made a rude gesture.

'He'll remember that if and when they catch up with us, cousin,' Drifter pointed out. He turned his gaze in another direction and received a surprise. 'Will you look into those trees on the hilltop, amigo?'

Almost directly above them, two of

Denver's posse had emerged from cover and taken in the chase already in progress. Within a minute, others joined them and soon the whole posse was lined up and watching the progress of the fugitives and the pursuing Mexicans.

'To be hunted by one group is bad enough,' Lopez grumbled, 'but two, that is too much!'

'I'm not sure I wouldn't rather be chased on American soil,' Drifter remarked, without conviction.

Long before they entered cover again, the American posse was swarming down the slope on a converging course with the Mexicans. The sight of them did nothing to give the fugitives confidence in the immediate future. Near the first of the tree belts which separated them from the winding track to the town, they slowed to a walk, so keen were they to know the outcome of the meeting of the two formidable forces.

Mexicans and Americans alike brandished their weapons as the gap narrowed, but no shots were fired. At last dismounted and in a position to rock their saddles, they watched the brief pause between their respective enemies.

Denver and Marshal O'Halloran on the one hand and two Mexicans on the other moved forward to parley over the situation. The gaunt buckskin-clad figure of the peace officer loomed tall in the saddle as he pointed after the runaways.

'Think they'll all come together?' Drifter wondered as he cinched up again.

Lopez spat upon his hands and rubbed them in the grass. He shook his head. 'See that, amigo? Money changin' hands. Denver is bribin' them to overlook the invasion of American police into the country. Two things will have reacted in the Americans' favour. They have numerical superiority, and they have offered money. An interesting combination.'

The Texican was not inclined to

hurry over mounting up again, but when he saw the whole party coming forward in two tight bunches he had second thoughts. The *rurales* were ahead, but only by a few yards. The pursuit was on again. The odds against their survival had increased. An anxious half hour of riding, partly in tree belts and partly in the open, brought them back to the trail which they sought.

As soon as they emerged upon it, they were forced to make a decision. To head straight for Perdido, or to make some sort of a diversion.

'Diversion? Pah!' Lopez spat into the eddying dust. 'Who can be sure anyone will come after us if we leave the trail again? The time for helpin' others is over. We have to fend for ourselves now. We have troubles enough!'

'I think we should try jest once more to lose some of our followers,' Drifter argued doggedly.

While they were arguing they continued up the trail. In fifty yards the quality of the going underfoot altered.

The surface of the track became markedly sandy. Lopez's mounting words of protest went over Drifter's head as he studied the way the horses' shoes threw up the sand.

'I'm goin' off trail on the east side, at least for a short distance, cousin. I hope you'll be at my back when I look around.'

Without waiting to check the impact of his words, he turned off trail and started weaving his way through fern and low clumps of scrub. For a minute, Lopez hesitated. Hoarse shouts from the rear finally helped him to make up his mind. He aimed a few salty oaths at the sky and leapt his roan off the trail.

★ ★ ★

Meanwhile, for inhabitants of the soulless and dispirited town of Perdido the early afternoon dragged on. Perhaps fifty of the families of the old town had still stayed on after the raid which had ended in the sacking of the church.

They kept themselves to themselves and occupied only the adobes to the south and west. No one ever went near the church, in the absence of a priest.

Ten or a dozen adobes towards the north and east side of the church and the square had become the temporary homes of squatters. The worst kind of drifters: white American and swarthy Mexican thieves, gunmen and knife throwers used it as a transit camp, at times harassing the local families; at other times they fought among themselves or endeavoured to wrest from more successful groups the money and valuables which they had captured in their travels.

Seven or eight Americans were tossing horseshoes in the long narrow shade afforded by a block of adobes. Not far off, a smaller rival gang of renegade Mexicans threw knives into a stuffed rounded target from a distance of forty feet. Further along the block, others too drunk or too tired to do otherwise stretched out in the shade and slept.

Presently, the sound of the hard-pushed team of shaft horses came to the ears of those who were most alert. The horseshoe game, however, was drawing to its climax, while the points were piling up in the Mexicans' knife-throwing contest.

Two whites and a Mexican strolled towards the approach track more out of curiosity than anything else. Small groups were often calling, many of them to pull out again more hastily than they appeared. But a wagon was something different. This one was to cause a surprise.

During the last half mile, Father Joseph had changed his clothes. Now, he strode forward ahead of the wagon dressed in a long black clerical habit, his flat parson's hat and a pair of open sandals. Clutched firmly in his right hand was the gold stone-encrusted crucifix. In his left was the chalice. His bearing and his expression showed great dignity and determination. He showed a total lack of fear or concern for those who came forward to inspect him.

Ernesto was up on the box, his women seated behind him. They, too, showed no special concern about the encroaching brigands. On they went, past the row of occupied adobes, with more and more of the undesirable squatters lining up to stare at them. The procession never faltered.

Ernesto headed his team straight for the church entrance, while the outlaws hung about, for the moment baffled. The American renegades did not seem to know how to act in these unusual circumstances, but right from the start the Mexicans behaved in a more circumspect fashion. Their dark eyes looked troubled as they eyed the formidable priest and the wagon crew behind him. Some among them started to cross themselves and back away.

Perhaps twenty of their number, mostly Americans, strolled along in the rear showing more curiosity than hostility. Eventually, Joseph reached the steps of the wooden church. He moved to the top of them and slowly turned to face those who followed. The wagon drew up to one side of him. The outlaws bunched together some twenty yards away, still disorganised and uncertain of themselves.

Ernesto jumped to the ground and assisted first Alicia and then Cipriana to get down. Without any show of fuss or nerves, they mounted the steps and grouped themselves beside the priest, waiting for him to speak. Joseph turned towards the outlaws, staring at them one after another with his piercing blue eyes. He cleared his throat.

He spoke in Spanish. 'See for yourselves, you who use this town for your own ends. The priceless treasures of this church have been recovered and will be used again. El Mestizo's sacking of this town has been his undoing. He has not lived to benefit from what he stole.

'Cuidad Nuevo is about to be restored to its former grace and dignity.

I have a word of warning for intruders. Change your ways and lead a God-fearing life from this time forward. Or go away from here.'

As the priest was talking a small Mexican boy ventured round the end of the building, coming from the still-populated area to the south. For a few moments, he stared as though unable to believe his eyes. The Carreras waved to him and gave him friendly smiles. He hopped from one foot to the other, did a couple of somersaults and suddenly ran off to tell others what he had seen.

'Hear me,' Joseph went on, 'where one innocent citizen has appeared others will appear. You will find the townsfolk hungry for respectability and willing to go to great lengths to restore their settlement. Their hope is about to be renewed, and with it their craving for a good life in a clean place.

'Those who return will want their homes back. There will be no room for those who misuse the church or the people. Take heed. Go from this place while the way is still open. Already men with guns are on their way here. The only habitation for wrong-doers who are slow to move will be in the cemetery! The posse is hunting outlaws at this very moment!'

Most of the Americans who heard his speech understood the gist of it. For the sake of those who were still uninformed, he repeated most of what he had said in the American tongue. All the time he was talking a grim smile played around the corners of his mouth.

At last he had finished. His expression became calm. He made the sign of the cross with the crucifix, bowed his head for a few moments and then stepped to the door. It swung open as he turned the handle. He stepped aside, ushering the family through it. When it closed there was an awful clanging sound which smote the ears of the hostile groups.

For a time, they hung about, angered and unsettled, clearly disturbed by the implied threats in the priest's words.

17

In the last mile before the town, Drifter and Lopez were back on trail and feeling desperate. Their last diversion had had the effect of drawing the *rurales* away to the east, but having outwitted the Mexican police on their own soil, they still had to deal with Denver and his posse. This was because the Americans had not embarked upon the last diversion. Instead, the riders from Rio City had been content to stay on the main trail and make steady progress for Perdido.

Consequently, when the partners re-emerged on the trail it was to find that the posse was only a few hundred yards behind them and, seemingly, nothing would deter them any more from moving solidly into the town where Joseph and his friends had gone. Perhaps they had guessed the truth about the whereabouts of the treasure. Even if they had not, the critical situation was too far advanced to do much about it.

Lopez was riding with the butt end of a cigar in his mouth. Unlike Drifter, he had the feeling that Perdido would be disastrous for them. In his innermost thoughts, Joseph's sketchy remarks about a possible reward for acting as guards for the wagon acted only to disturb him.

He had been the one who wanted a big and just reward against all other considerations. Now, he was not so sure. The protracted riding ahead of numerous determined enemies was getting him down. Although he did not want to admit it, he had a hankering to make a detour and keep going on it, giving Perdido the widest berth possible in an attempt to prolong their liberty.

The dryness of his throat made him cough. The cigar butt shot out of his mouth and was seen to bounce off a small eroded rock. He gave vent to his feelings in fast elided Spanish.

'Does it occur to you that we might have enemies at this very moment on three sides of us, cousin? A man who likes freedom as much as you do ought to take the one alternative open to him. Ride towards the west an' keep going.'

'Cousin, for quite a while now, I've had the feelin' that we are caught up in something bigger than ourselves. Something greatly worthwhile. I want to go forward an' see Father Joseph make good in that town he thinks so much about. I wouldn't want to slip back into the States without knowin' exactly what is happenin'. Would you?'

Lopez gave no straight answer. His jeering laugh was back on his face. The one which, when he was drunk, prompted so much ill-feeling.

'Doggone it, cousin, you're taken with the girl! Why don't you admit it?'

'All right, so I admit it. What's so wrong about that? You ride west, if you want to. Me, I'm goin' on. But before I get there, I'm goin' to fire off a few angry shots at the posse to slow them up. Doggone it, they've had things far too easy since they chased us across the big river!'

Once again, Drifter forced the sorrel ahead and left Lopez to make a hasty decision. The Texan was soon negotiating the last big bend before the snaking approach track towards the settlement. Bulking on the right was a thickly-grassed hill, capped by stunted trees. Lopez was almost at his shoulder again when he pointed to a narrow animal track leading to the top.

'I'm goin' up there to fire off a few shots at the posse! You can stay here if you feel like it. My mind is made up.'

Clutching his Winchester tightly in one hand, Drifter began the ascent. Within a few yards, he had the notion that this last move was a foolhardy one. He was tired. Lopez was tired. Even if they succeeded in slowing the posse, the brief respite was not likely to do anyone any material good in the town. He toiled on, however, and threw himself down in the yielding grass with perspiration starting from his forehead and all the way around his hatband.

The posse appeared, moving at a walking pace, just as Lopez flopped down beside him. 'The Apaches would have done a better job than us, cousin,' the Texican remarked breathlessly.

Drifter pointed out Denver, O'Halloran and Kilbride, riding just ahead of the Block brothers in their derby hats. The rest followed on in threes and fours.

'The aim is not to kill,' Drifter cautioned. 'Only to slow them up a little. After this, we think only of ourselves an' Perdido.'

Drifter fired the first shot. It chipped stones between the legs of Denver's gelding. Lopez playfully lined up his weapon on Marshal O'Halloran's big hat, but he did not fire it at the peace officer. As soon as the first shell was discharged, the Texan had rolled a few yards to one side before firing again. He was trying really hard to make the posse men think there were more than two hostile rifles. Grudgingly, Lopez gave his support for a scheme he did not approve. Lowering his sights, he fired close enough in front of the marshal's great black mount to make it rear up and drop him on the trail. Denver's gelding had danced sideways into Kilbride's stallion making the latter horse prance away into the bushes.

The partners continued to fire, lever and shift their positions until their magazines were empty. By that time, all the riders had scattered and taken cover. Only O'Halloran's black stayed on trail and it was galloping in the wrong direction.

'That ought to do the trick,' Drifter murmured. 'Let's go!'

He wriggled backwards as two or three ranging shots flew back at them from the trail. As soon as he deemed it safe, he rose to his feet and started down the narrow track again. Lopez dallied for a few seconds, more out of curiosity than anything else.

Drifter was down at trail level and

Lopez scrambling down behind him when a high-pitched tinny-sounding bell began to peal in the town. The sound carried well and filled the young Texan's mind with fresh conjecture. He leapt into the saddle and waited for Lopez to come up with him.

'Church bells, amigo! If that sound doesn't convince you our friends are makin' progress nothin' else will! Let's ride!'

'All right, so we ride,' Lopez agreed, 'but don't go buildin' up your hopes. Anybody can ring church bells. It doesn't have to mean anything very special.'

Side by side, they hustled their horses forward, chancing many a backward glance in case any curious posse man was far enough forward to catch a glimpse of them. No one showed up.

'They'll be along quite soon,' Lopez prophesied pessimistically. 'Havin' come this far, a few hostile shots off a hilltop won't hold them for long. Neither will the church bells!'

Drifter ignored him. His racing thoughts told him that Father Joseph was in charge of the town, and that meant that the Carreras had survived; that Cipriana had suffered no hurt. He called for all the sorrel's last remaining stamina and went ahead.

Three minutes later, a bunch of horsemen came towards them from the town, riding with urgency. Only a few seconds' observation was necessary to identify them as killers and thieves. The cousins reacted instantly, turning sharply off trail to westwards, hoping fervently that the riders coming from town had not seen them.

Masked by trailside rocks and a pair of pine trees, they awaited the next development. 'I told you not everybody likes church bells, cousin. Something sure as hell is happenin' back there, but I for one would not like to predict what it is.'

Practically all of the first bunch of outlaws had the rig and stamp of Mexicans. They thundered on by, and were followed by an even bigger bunch of American renegades a few seconds later. Drifter was aware that they were still in striking distance of the posse. He therefore dismounted and walked the sorrel at a steady pace, using the trailside rocks for cover. Lopez followed him, directly behind.

Another, smaller group of riders came thundering round the bend. By that time, Drifter was too curious to maintain walking progress. He mounted up again and went forward on trail, keen and watchful. A sudden series of gun exchanges downtrail made them stiffen. The first bunch of renegades had ridden directly into the posse.

Lopez was sufficiently distracted to ride back and see the outcome, but Drifter pushed ahead and he had perforce to follow or lose contact. Soon they were on the last gradient. No more riders came towards them, but on either hand silent Mexicans with rifles, revolvers and almost every kind of known weapon rose out of cover and menaced them.

There was now no turning back. Side by side, they rode through the stern eyed swarthy-skinned gunmen. Many weapons pointed directly at them, but none were fired. On the outskirts of the town itself, upwards of three score Mexicans barred their way, seemingly at variance with the strident notes of the church bell.

'We are friends of Father Joseph!' Drifter called hoarsely.

The ring of guns closed in steadily. Lopez said the same sentence in Spanish, and still there were no friendly faces. Due to their height in the saddles, they could see women and children grouped beyond the men. Just when all seemed lost, a familiar female figure detached itself from the others and ran down the hill past the first adobes.

She called first in Spanish. Her words had an immediate effect. Expressions on faces changed, and weapons turned away.

Cipriana called: 'You made it! Welcome to Perdido, Drifter! And you too Lopez!'

A path opened to the horses. She

came through it without effort and reached up to Drifter who caught her in his arms and raised her into the saddle before him. A polite murmur ran through the throng of revitalised locals who had rallied to free their town and support their priest.

Cipriana started to babble about how the local families had driven out the outlaws by their sudden show of unity and strength, but Drifter stemmed her flow of words with a passionate kiss, closely followed by a warning about the approaching American posse. A few choice suggestions by the girl caused the assembled armed men to fall back upon the church, where Father Joseph was located. Willing hands led the tired horses, even hauling them along to the focal point.

As they neared the building, the bell stopped ringing and they were left with just the echoes. The priest emerged with a radiant expression on his face as they dismounted. He shook them warmly by the hand and thanked them.

Then, from the sleeves of his clerical habit he produced two brown envelopes and handed one to each of them.

'Your pay, my friends, for acting as guards to our very precious properties. Now you are free to go, or you may stay. The townspeople and I are capable of handling the posse and any other eventualities which crop up. If you decide to go, I for one, will be disappointed.'

His glance travelled as far as Cipriana, who blushed. She elected to show them the interior of the church, while Joseph made ready to confront yet another bunch of angry men. The building smelled damp and was covered in dust, but the girl showed no signs of displeasure.

Drifter took her hand and mounted the wooden steps to the bell tower. Lopez plodded along behind, for once wrapped up in his own thoughts. By time they reached the open sides of the tower and were able to see out, Denver and his men were walking their horses towards the church. The wagon had earlier been shifted west of the church, and by straining a little Drifter could see that their horses had also been taken into the small square at the rear of the church. Willing hands had already started to groom them by a pump.

Upwards of one hundred male Mexicans now formed up on either side of the walking posse, headed by Denver, O'Halloran, Kilbride and the brothers Block. They had hidden their hostility along with their weapons. Backed by women and children, no one in the posse thought of them as a force to be reckoned with.

O'Halloran began the exchanges by glowering down at the priest.

'Father, this posse has travelled a long way to recapture a wrong-doer who robbed a bank in Rio City. You have the authority. I demand you produce this man, Lopez, an' his pardner.'

Joseph stared him out. 'You have no jurisdiction in Mexico. In riding into this town as you did, you have broken the law. There are no undesirables in this town other than yourselves.'

Denver's legs were twitching as anger possessed him. 'Strong words for a priest,' he challenged. 'I seek to recover the box and its contents which was stolen by the thief Lopez. I believe you have it here. We shall take it by force, if necessary.'

Joseph nodded calmly: 'You are Mark Denver, the banker motivated by avarice. Know then that the box you seek was the property of my brother. He also was a priest. He was murdered in this church by El Mestizo, whose treasure you seek to claim for your own. The crucifix, the chalice and the sum of fifty thousand dollars all belong to this church and this community. They have been restored. Depart, and seek forgiveness for your sins. I would not trust you with any funds of mine.'

Joseph turned away, as though to re-enter the church. Overhead, Lopez drew a revolver and aimed it at the head of the banker. Drifter had great difficulty in restraining him from firing it. He had to pin his cousin to the ground and twist his arm. 'You fool, Joseph has just said all undesirables have left town. Do you want to make him a liar?' Lopez thought about the implications and gave in.

'You're bluffing, priest,' Denver called harshly.

On either side and behind him, the men taking Denver's pay drew their weapons and aimed them at the solitary black-garbed figure. Before the priest had sufficient time to turn and face the threat a mighty change came over the assembled male Mexicans. Suddenly they were armed and very much on the alert. Menaced by five times as many guns as they possessed, the mounted men of the posse capitulated. Their guns were hastily holstered again.

'We can offer you a good Christian burial if you so wish it,' Joseph observed.

But Denver had given in. The posse left. Not a shot was fired.

That night there was feasting, music and joy in the town. The two American cousins were much fêted. Drifter had never known such a time. He danced with Cipriana until wine and weariness called a halt. Drifter was put to bed in the same adobe as his cousin. They slept late.

One day later, Lopez left the village alone. Drifter was distressed but he had no inclination to follow him. He went for a long horse ride with his intended and when he came back he consulted Father Joseph, whose time was taken up with the settling in of returning families.

Joseph received the young couple in his vestry. 'Lopez will be back,' he promised, 'when he has finished spending his thousand dollars. He will come back because he needs your company and is little use on his own. I think he will be back in time for the wedding.'

Drifter, toying with his hat, was about

to enquire who was to be married. Cipriana, however, knew exactly what Joseph meant. She blushed and started to chuckle. Drifter perceived that the nuptials were to be his own. He grinned broadly, knowing it was high time he made his proposal and asked for his friend's advice.

★   ★   ★

In time, Joseph's notions about Lopez were proved correct.

THE END

We do hope that you have enjoyed reading this large print book.

Did you know that all of our titles are available for purchase?

We publish a wide range of high quality large print books including:
Romances, Mysteries, Classics
General Fiction
Non Fiction and Westerns

Special interest titles available in large print are:
The Little Oxford Dictionary
Music Book, Song Book
Hymn Book, Service Book

Also available from us courtesy of Oxford University Press:
Young Readers' Dictionary
(large print edition)
Young Readers' Thesaurus
(large print edition)

For further information or a free brochure, please contact us at:
Ulverscroft Large Print Books Ltd.,
The Green, Bradgate Road, Anstey,
Leicester, LE7 7FU, England.
Tel: (00 44) **0116 236 4325**
Fax: (00 44) **0116 234 0205**

Other titles in the
Linford Western Library:

JUST BREATHIN' HATE

Dempsey Clay

When the Law went loco and charged him with killing his wife, innocent Jack Fallon had two choices only — run or hang. So he ran — to a strange lost valley shut off from the world and ruled by a cult of holy men who would prove more lethal than any posse could ever be . . .

THE FENCE BUSTERS

Tom Gordon

The open Texas range was the finest cattle-land in the world. But when some forward thinking men erected fences, others suffered the consequences as their cattle were deprived of water and the best grassland. These men turned night-riders, destroying the long fence lines. Lives were lost and property ruined . . . Young and reckless, Tom Midnight joined the ranks of the fencers; his flaming guns were there to argue with the eastern speculators, seeking to fan the flames of conflict.